GROWER'S MARKET

GROWER'S MARKET

A Novel of Free Enterprise in Marijuana Country

MICHAEL BAUGHMAN

Skyhorse Publishing

Skyhorse Publishing books may be purchased in bulk at special discounts for sales promotion, corporate gifts, fund-raising, or educational purposes. Special editions can also be created to specifications. For details, contact the Special Sales Department, Skyhorse Publishing, 307 West 36th Street, 11th Floor, New York, NY 10018 or info@skyhorsepublishing.com.

Skyhorse® and Skyhorse Publishing® are registered trademarks of Skyhorse Publishing, Inc.®, a Delaware corporation.

Visit our website at www.skyhorsepublishing.com

10 9 8 7 6 5 4 3 2 1

Library of Congress Cataloging-in-Publication Data
is available on file.

Print ISBN: 978-1-63220-639-8
Ebook ISBN: 978-1-63220-795-1

Printed in the United States of America

This book is dedicated to the memory of Robert, Tommy, and Curtis

Doomed enterprises divide lives forever into the then and the now.

Cormac McCarthy, *The Crossing*

Many thanks to my editor, Lilly Golden, whose invaluable advice, as well as her patience, made telling this story possible.

CONTENTS

WE SHOULD KILL

HEADQUARTERS

This was the only tavern for sixty miles as the crow flies in any direction. Except for the big neon sign held between metal stanchions protruding from its roof the Bird of Prey looked like an oversized two-story log cabin. On a clear night the red and yellow sign depicting a hawk clutching a fat long-tailed mouse in its talons could be seen from half a mile either way along the two-lane road. The structure had been built by a German immigrant named Eisenkopf in 1897 with the ground floor serving as a combination general store and blacksmith shop and Herr and Frau Eisenkopf living above. Soon after Eisenkopf died of influenza in 1919 his widow sold the building to a cowboy who turned it into an auction house for horses. By the time the cowboy died there was insufficient local demand for horses so the cowboy's son opened a rooming house, but soon after that he was drafted into the army and killed at war. Back home his young widow established the Bird of Prey tavern with apartments to rent on the top floor. She eventually remarried and gave birth to a son who was named Drum after his father. At eighteen Drum Junior married a San Francisco hippie girl known as Sunbeam and two months after the wedding his father tracked a bull elk through newly fallen snow in October and stumbled over a fallen *log and shot himself through the heart. When Drum Junior's mother died he and Sunbeam took over the Bird of Prey. In late middle-age Drum Junior suffered a fatal heart attack and since then Sunbeam has run the tavern herself.*

The parking lot was crowded mostly with pickups and SUVs, and inside the big room was almost full. Patrons came from many miles away and from all directions and this was the happy time on a Saturday night when nearly everyone who would be there had arrived and nobody was thinking about leaving yet.

Shadow and Shrimp had the two stools at the end of the long bar not far from a jukebox that sat directly between the restroom doors. Without a television set in the Bird of Prey the jukebox was the only entertainment in the place. Shrimp sat at the end of the bar with Shadow, next to a middle-aged fat man wearing a camouflage cowboy hat with a rattlesnake band. The fat cowboy was drinking shots of tequila and the young men had pint glasses of amber ale in front of them.

Shadow had served with Shrimp through three tours in a recent war but now after their service the two created disparate appearances. Shadow had kept his army crew cut and clean shave while Shrimp had grown a head of curly black hair, which hung down past his shoulders, and a thick beard that reached nearly halfway to his waist. The beard covered some of the plastic surgery scars on his face and the visible scars showed white against his suntan. Shadow wore jeans and a clean gray hooded sweatshirt, and Shrimp wore faded camouflage army fatigues.

Shadow was thinking about rumors he had been hearing and about the three men they had caught and beaten out in the woods that day and the old man who might have escaped when a lovely young blond woman in faded jeans and a tight black blouse walked up to the jukebox and stood there with her head tilted to one side pondering selections.

"Nice ass," Shadow said to Shrimp.

"Looks like a college girl," Shrimp answered.

"Think so?"

"All I know is old Uncle Sam wanted college. He'd be good as gold right now if he never thought about a college, but look at the poor son of a bitch. All I know is the only reason almost anybody goes to a college is so they can maybe make more money later on, an' I say fuck that, it's bullshit. We make mighty good money without college, right? We already got enough to open up our own place whenever we want, right?"

"All I know is you got at least two things that're all you know."

"It pisses me off is all. Just look what wantin' college did to Uncle Sam. Don't talk college to me."

"I hear you," Shadow answered.

"All I know is that's what I mean."

Finally the blond dropped her coins into the slot and pushed some buttons and turned and walked away through the crowd.

"*Awesome* ass," Shrimp said.

"Until we open up our own place maybe we got to hit some new tavern once in a while," Shadow said. "Where there's better things to do than check out asses."

"Like where?"

"Some dude's opening a strip club out there by Four Corners."

"Who?"

"Just some dude who inherited money."

"But that's eighty goddamn miles away."

"We got vehicles," Shadow said. "Toon told me about it this afternoon. It'll open up by the end of the year and they figure to have these special nights scheduled. Like Amateur Night. Wet T-shirt Night. Whipped Cream Night. Men's Night. Stuff like that."

"Men's Night?"

"Yeah. The men'll strip and the women can bid on the ones they like. I guess it'll be a way to get women in the place."

"Or keep women out. Or maybe Toon can strip and the women who dig tattoos can bid on him. Maybe I could go for Whipped Cream Night though."

"Me too. Whatever the hell it is."

Shadow's glass was nearly empty now and he lifted it slowly and took a long swallow of the lukewarm ale.

The jukebox ballad about a long-haul truck driver was sung slightly off-key in a high soprano voice with a Southern accent accompanied by an electric guitar.

"That song definitely sucks," Shrimp said, "but I'm gonna look that little blond college lady up right about now."

He got up and carried his ale through the crowd toward the booths on the far side of the room.

5

SHADOW

Shadow had grown up an only child whose father was a preacher in a fishing town on the nearby coast. The preacher believed with all his evangelical heart that the earth was 6,000 years old and that there had been a man named Noah who single-handedly built and sailed an ark and that the worst man on earth was far superior to the finest woman (if there was a finest woman) and that all homosexuals and Jews and niggers and spics and chinks and japs and dagos and ragheads and adulterers among various other groups of misfits and perverts were doomed to what he visualized and preached about as the gigantic and eternal frying pan in the immense barbecue pit of hell. Beginning at age six Shadow had accompanied his father to homes where the preacher knelt and prayed aloud over the bodies of the recently deceased beseeching God to allow them through the pearly gates (that was what he called them) into paradise (that was what he called it). Shadow always stood a few feet behind his father staring at the corpses. Some were covered all the way over their heads by sheets or blankets and some weren't. He had seen dozens of dead bodies including several children before he went off to war. During his time as a soldier he saw hundreds of dead men and many women and children and soon hardened himself to it. Then, after his discharge, while driving a logging road on only his third day back home he rounded a turn and hit a deer. The young glassy-eyed bleating doe lay on her side just in front of the pickup truck with her spindly legs kicking feebly. A fractured lower hind leg flopped spasmodically and raised small clouds of fine brown dust. Five bloated ticks showed on the doe's smooth white belly. To put the animal out of her misery Shadow killed her with a tire iron. He struck the doe on the top of the head between the ears until first the bleating stopped and then the legs no longer moved. It took what seemed a long time and the head had become a bloody bony mushy hairy pulp with bulging eyes. Shadow dragged the carcass off the road and turned the truck around and drove back home. The dead doe bothered him more than any dead human ever had. When he related what had happened and what he had had to do and how depressed it had made him his father explained that animals didn't really matter because only God and white men did, and he pounded his big fist on the kitchen tabletop as he spoke. The vivid image of the dead doe's head remained in Shadow's mind, and two weeks later he took off and headed toward a new life in the old pickup. He was broke and anguished and alone, and he wished it had been his father's head instead.

Shadow didn't watch Shrimp search for the pretty blond. He drained his glass and waved at the bartender who smiled at him and waved back as she set mixed drinks in tall glasses on the bar for a young couple sitting a few stools away. Then she stepped to the end of the bar and stood in front of Shadow and he smiled back at her. She was somewhere close to thirty years old and trim and pretty with long dark hair worn in a ponytail tied with a bright red ribbon.

"Hello, Rainbow," Shadow said.

"Hey, Shadow. One more pint?"

"Yes please. Hey. How's Uncle Sam?"

"Oh, you know. The same."

"Hey, I heard on the news the VA might shape up some."

"That'll be the day."

"Right," Shadow said. "Should I go up and look in on him tonight?"

"You could try. He might be asleep. Probably is. He likes it when you visit. I can tell."

"Hey Rainbow!" a man called from somewhere down the bar. Rainbow ignored him. "I'll bring your pint," she told Shadow.

"Gracias."

"Shrimp too?"

"He took his glass with him but I think he needs one."

Soon after Rainbow carried Shadow's empty glass away, Shrimp returned to his barstool. "That sweet blond thing's with some huge dude, some asshole who's half drunk," he said. "I mean *huge.* I almost had to coldcock the ignorant shithead. Somebody'll kick his ass before the night's over, I guarantee you that. Or somebody'll try. I sure do hope to see that little lady again sometime. It's her first time here she said."

"Rainbow's bringing us pints. Want to head upstairs and check on Uncle Sam?"

"Soon as the pints arrive."

Rainbow served the pints of amber ale topped with an inch of rich white foam.

Shadow took a long drink. He liked the feel of the cold wet glass in his hand.

Shrimp handed a ten-dollar bill across the bar and Rainbow took it and smiled but was too busy filling orders to stop and talk.

GROWER'S MARKET

Both men stood with pints in hand. "I guess we'll lose our bar spots," Shrimp said.

"Fuck it," Shadow answered. "We'll squeeze back in somewhere."

As he swallowed ale Shadow noticed the fat man in the cowboy hat punching numbers into a cell phone.

"That thing won't work around here," he said to the cowboy.

"What?"

"I said that thing won't work around here."

"I got service five miles down the road."

"You're five miles up the road now, dude."

"Well, that pretty much sucks."

"We kind of like it out of range," Shrimp said. "Could be you're in the wrong place."

"It fucking sucks," the cowboy answered.

"Could be you suck," Shrimp said. "Hey, would you save us our stools while we're gone?"

The fat cowboy squinted out from underneath his hat as if he were looking into a bright light, and then he looked away and slid his cell phone back into his shirt pocket with one hand and picked up his empty shot glass with the other. When he looked into the glass he appeared to be surprised to see it was empty.

RAINBOW

One late night at the bar Shadow had told Rainbow about killing the doe with the tire iron and how his father the preacher had driven him from home and finally to this place, and the story surprised her.

Rainbow had left Texas because of her daddy. (Nearly all Texas kids call their fathers "daddy.") Rainbow's daddy had illegal Mexicans working at menial jobs on the ranch so she heard Spanish growing up and learned the language easily. The Mexican men worked hard for meager wages in all weather through every season of the year, and the women and children who worked hard to help the men received no pay. All the Mexicans liked Rainbow because she spoke their language, but one day her daddy overheard her call out "Hola" to a little girl on the ranch and he gave Rainbow a dirty look and took off his white Stetson hat and shook his shiny bald head and spat and walked away. "Can't my goddamn daughter talk American?" he called back over his shoulder. On a hot humid summer morning Rainbow walked into a bank with her daddy and he stepped up to a counter where a small wooden sign said "Habla Espanol." Her daddy asked the Mexican man behind the counter if his name was Habla and the man smiled and shook his head no and her daddy asked him why he had the sign there if that wasn't even his name and then called him a stupid beaner. There were many such incidents through the years, and the day after high school graduation Rainbow left her home and her town and the state of Texas forever.

"Drop Kick Me Jesus Through the Goal Posts of Life" by Bobby Bare was playing on the jukebox as Shadow and Shrimp threaded their way through the crowd and across the room and then through a narrow doorway and finally up a dark flight of stairs.

At the top of the stairway they opened a door and walked into Rainbow's three-room apartment. It was the smallest of the four apartments on the second floor. They walked across the dark living room and into the dimly lit bedroom where Rainbow's husband Uncle Sam lay flat on his back on a single bed against the wall by a window that looked out over the crowded parking lot. Red had always been Uncle Sam's favorite color, and the walls and ceiling in the room had been painted blood red and a red rug lay on the floor and red curtains framed the small window.

Uncle Sam had lost both arms and both legs to an "improvised explosive device." The arms were gone above his elbows and the legs well above his knees. The blast had ruined his brain and paralyzed his torso from the neck down. He couldn't move and couldn't speak, but when spoken to could sometimes blink his eyes. Sometimes he could chew soft foods and swallow liquids when Rainbow fed him.

Three metal folding chairs also painted red were leaned against the red wall near the door Shadow and Shrimp had entered by. Shadow handed Shrimp his ale. He opened two of the chairs and carried one in each hand and placed them close to the bed and he and Shrimp sat down.

Uncle Sam wore a red T-shirt and lay covered up to his chest with a red quilt with his arm stumps underneath the quilt. His pillowcase was red and his eyes were narrowly opened and reflected light from the blinking red and yellow neon sign outside and he showed no indication he realized Shadow and Shrimp were there.

"Hey, buddy," Shadow said.

"Hello, Uncle Sam," Shrimp said. "Crowded downstairs tonight. Hunters, rednecks, growers, all kinds. Ol' Rainbow's mighty busy."

The narrowly opened eyes didn't blink.

"He might hear us all the time," Shadow said. "Just because he doesn't blink doesn't mean he can't hear us."

"He might never hear us," Shrimp answered. "Just because he blinks doesn't mean he *can* hear us either."

"It'd be better if he didn't hear us. I guess it'd be a whole hell of a lot better if he never heard anything. But maybe he does." Shadow patted Uncle Sam's shoulder. "We'll give you some brew here in a while," he said. "Good stuff. Amber ale."

"It's fall," Shrimp said. "In the old days we'd be out there in deer camp by now. Remember sitting around the fire at night in camp? Sipping a little Jim Beam and bullshitting? Was that *sweet*? Anyway, we saw a six-point yesterday. The dumbass was in easy range and stood there staring at us. Like he wanted to walk on over and talk. Up there by Tubbs Springs. We didn't shoot him though. But he's a dumbass and somebody sure as shit will. We don't shoot deer anymore. Just people if we got to. Like they trained us to do."

They both stared at Uncle Sam's face as they talked. He was dark-haired and pale-skinned and gaunt now but still handsome. They'd both been to Uncle Sam's and Rainbow's wedding before their war. Shadow had been best man and the wedding had been in the deer camp clearing in the woods out by the east fork of Jump Off Joe Creek. A big crowd was there. Lots of people got stoned and a few got drunk. After the war started they'd both tried to talk Uncle Sam out of enlisting with them, but the logging jobs were gone and Uncle Sam said he needed the money for college and the army was the only way he could get it and this that they saw under the red quilt on the bed was what he got instead.

"We got us an excellent crop this year," Shrimp said. "Super first-class prime cannabis. But there's rumors some outsiders might show up to rip us off. I guess we got a few rippers around already. Saw some today in fact. Dealt with 'em. Some dude named Crazy Carlos might show up later somebody said. It's all rumors though. Always is. Nobody knows what the fuck's really going on."

"We heard this dude Crazy Carlos used to be a porn star," Shadow added. "Shrimp here and me figure we'll cut out and open up our restaurant pretty soon. It'll be a first-class place too. All we got to do is figure what kind of food to serve. What kind of cuisine. We been watching that Food Channel every Thursday. That channel's tough to find, out in the sticks, so we got to drive big miles to see the son of a bitch, but we hardly ever miss it."

"He's right," Shrimp said. "There's too many crazy motherfuckers out here all over the mountains, more all the time. We got our loot all saved, more than enough loot, and pretty soon we'll do it. Maybe we'll figure it all out after we take our winter vacations. Maybe this'll be our last season out here."

"First-class cuisine!" Shadow said. "The total opposite of army chow!" He patted Uncle Sam's shoulder. "You wait, dude! You'll be a fucking guest of honor! We'll get you in there soon as we open the doors!"

Uncle Sam didn't blink.

Shrimp changed the subject. "Used to be all we did in fall was hunt," he said. "Remember how we used to sit in camp maybe blowing some weed along with the Jim Beam around the camp-fire? Remember that humongous buck you got that year when you slept late and everybody else was hunting in the old home-stead draw and that dumb fuck walked right past the tent right after you crawled out of your fart sack? How come so many deer are so fucking dumb?"

Uncle Sam's eyes didn't blink. Shadow patted his shoulder again and then slid his free hand underneath Uncle Sam's head and slowly lifted his head up. It felt heavy. With the head close to vertical he positioned the low edge of his pint glass between Uncle Sam's slightly parted lips. "Here's some beer," he said. "I mean some amber ale. You ready, buddy? Swallow it down now. Here it comes, dude."

When Shadow carefully tilted the glass the beer dribbled down Uncle Sam's chin onto his neck and the collar of his T-shirt. Dark stains appeared on the red material.

"I think maybe he's asleep," Shrimp said.

Shadow slowly lowered the heavy head back down onto the red pillow.

"We should kill him," Shrimp said. "He'd be way better off, right?"

"What if he hears you say that?"

"I feel so fucking sorry for Rainbow."

"She doesn't want us to kill him."

"When was the last time you asked her?"

"A while back. A few months I guess."

"Just because she says she doesn't want us to doesn't really mean she doesn't want us to. You think?"

"No," Shadow said. "She just can't say it is all."

"Well then we should. We could do it right now. We could do it with the pillow. Rainbow ever tell you how she wants to be a nurse someday?"

"Yeah, she told me. She got the idea from that old lady who died, that nurse named Heather."

"Well she could do it if we helped Uncle Sam here die."

"She might really not want us to kill him though."

"Talk to her again."

"I will. But she won't be able to say it. How can we know for sure?"

Shadow used the sleeve of his sweatshirt to blot the beer from Uncle Sam's chin and neck. Then they sat for a while sipping the amber ale and looking down at him.

"Talk to her again for sure," Shrimp said. "Ask her at least."

"I will."

UNCLE SAM

"Hold the pickles, hold the lettuce,
special orders don't upset us."

The eleven words of doggerel began sounding through Uncle Sam's mind the first time Rainbow waited on him at Burger King all those years ago. He had never given a thought to what people called "love at first sight" and then it happened to him. In her silly Burger King uniform she was lovely with wide brown eyes and long black hair and a lithe and sexy figure and a smile that showed she was happy despite her work. All of that was clear at first sight. But Uncle Sam thought he saw even more there and he was right. They married a little less than six months after she served him his first Whopper. From grade school through high school and then at work Uncle Sam had been confident and talented and smart. He had been a success on the basketball court and in the classroom and then as a part-time logger. With Rainbow he found his happiness and four months after their wedding his troop plane landed overseas and exactly one month later on a hot summer morning he was riding in a Hummer along a narrow dusty road through a barren valley between two steep brown mountains and there came a blinding white flash and roaring heat and instantaneous oblivion.

"Hold the pickles, hold the lettuce, special orders don't upset us."

In what remained of his mind he heard it yet today.

BASEBALL CAPS

CASE

When Case thought of his wife he understood that even though she had died in that awful way the pity he felt wasn't nearly so much for her as for himself. Heather had been a nurse in his war and had cared for him after he suffered his wounds. They fell in love and kidded about how they were just like Catherine Barkley and Frederic Henry in A Farewell to Arms. *Like* Hemingway's couple they hated the war and after Case was as healed as he would ever be and then Heather's discharge seven months later they married and soon moved to the woods where Case cruised timber for the Forest Service. He used whiskey and marijuana in moderation to deal with his pain and from spring through fall he and Heather fly-fished and cross-country skied and hunted grouse and mountain quail and hiked. Heather worked as a nurse for an old country doctor who practiced in a small town forty miles away. She had stitched wounds and set broken bones and delivered babies and finally retired after the old doctor died and no young doctor could be found to replace him. After her retirement she helped the bartender Rainbow care for her comatose husband at the Bird of Prey. Besides her nursing she enjoyed doing everything Case did except for the marijuana. She had nothing against marijuana but feared that using it *might somehow diminish its value to her husband. In the wintertime they both read books and listened to music and talked about what they had read and heard. They had no children and wanted none. They had agreed on that the first time they talked about marriage before they ever made love.*

When Case woke up in the cold and dark he had no idea where he was or what had happened to him. All he knew for certain was that he was alive. He felt nauseous and hungry at the same time and he tasted sour bile in his mouth, and even though his hands and feet were numb with the cold he could feel the wet earth caked underneath his fingernails.

He coughed and vomited and then remembered. The afternoon flashed into his mind with images clearer than truth. He had hiked across the wet green valley and was starting up the long hill when he heard men screaming in the woods behind him. At least three different voices were screaming words but they were too far away for any of it to be understood.

After a minute's pause there was loud screaming closer to him.

Case picked up his pace and soon he was panting for breath. The screaming came closer all the time and now he could discern some words:

"Motherfucking thieves!"

"Cocksuckers!"

When he looked back he saw nothing but trees. Now the hill was so steep that he had to pull himself up the slope by grasping sword ferns hand over hand. He stopped long enough to slide the straps of his backpack off his shoulders and down over his arms, and he heard the pack thud to the ground and then he kept climbing.

When a fern dislodged by the roots he fell heavily backward and cursed. He lay still for a moment and then rolled over and pushed himself up and resumed climbing. On a patch of damp pine needles his right foot slipped out from underneath him and he sprawled face-first onto the forest floor. He tasted warm blood in his mouth and his heart thudded heavily.

When he pushed himself to his feet he saw a huge fallen sugar pine blocking his path. Using limbs as handholds he tried climbing over the tree but the limbs weren't spaced to allow him to make it all the way over the top. On his fourth and final try he gashed the palm of his right hand on a splintered limb.

He spat a mouthful of blood and rubbed blood from his hand onto his pants and made his way around the pine instead of over it. His cotton shirt was stuck to his back with sweat. On the other side of the pine there was steeper terrain and he labored upward slower all the time as he fought through ferns and thick brush and wove back and forth among the big trees.

"*Assholes!*"

"*Motherfuckers!*"

The words echoed back from distant hills and as the echoes faded Case reached a place where the trunks of the trees had been scarred by fire and the brush grew sparsely. Not far ahead he saw a clearing and just beyond it an immense gray boulder that marked the summit.

On his hands and knees he crawled up to the base of the boulder and then scrambled around it and then all the way to the top where he lay facedown on smooth cool stone. His left thigh had cramped and he heard his rasping breath and tasted more blood in his mouth and swallowed it down.

A red-tail hawk soaring over the valley screeched.

A moment later a raven cawed from down below.

When Case heard the two birds he opened his eyes in time to see three men at least a quarter mile away. Even with his eyes deteriorated from age he could make out their black baseball caps and camouflage T-shirts and brown shorts and black boots. They ran hard across the valley floor with one of the men a few yards ahead of the other two. Then five more men came out of the trees not far behind the three. The five wore blue jeans and sweatshirts and the five soon caught the three. First the three were punched and then they were thrown to the ground and kicked, and Case could hear the hard kicks landing against flesh and bone and he heard the victims moan and beg. Their voices carried clearly up the long valley.

"We're sorry!" one of them said. *"Please, man, we're fuckin' sorry!"*

"Fuck you!" came the answer.

"Please stop! We're sorry fuckin' sorry please stop!"

"Fuck you!"

Soon the three men lay there sprawled out and motionless. Two lay on their backs and the other lay facedown, and Case heard boots thudding into the limp bodies.

The T-shirts the three downed men wore were stained darkly with blood and their faces were bloody too and their baseball caps lay nearby on the green grass.

Case heard one of the five men standing around the bodies say, "I think there's another motherfucker up ahead there somewhere. I think I saw another one way out ahead of us. Let's go."

Case watched the men enter the trees below him and heard them talking. He couldn't understand the words but he heard them moving up the hill and breaking through patches of brush and drawing closer.

Then they were close enough so he could understand.

"You sure there's another motherfucker?"

"I'm not sure. Maybe and maybe not."

"Can't you count? How fuckin' many did you see?"

"I'm not sure, asshole."

"In other words you can't count."

"Fuck you, Shrimp! Maybe there's one more. I thought I saw one. A cotton top. Some old dude."

The hawk screeched.

"Thought you saw some old dude. Fuck you, Shakespeare."

The raven cawed.

"We got to make sure."

"I'm tired, man. I'm wiped out. I'm ready for some beer."

"We're goin' up to the top of this hill first."

"What about the ones down below?"

"What about 'em? They learned their lesson."

"Fuckin' A!"

Case rolled onto his back and slid feet first off the boulder.

When he stood a wave of dizziness hit him so hard that he had to stand still with his head down and his hands on his knees and his eyes squeezed shut. He counted to ten in his mind and the first thing he saw when he opened his eyes was his right hand smeared with bright red blood.

He started down the hill careful to make no noise and soon he was back into big trees and no longer heard the voices. He was light-headed and feeling sick but he feared they might come after him and veered off to his left into a thick dark stand of Douglas firs.

Not far into the firs he came to another fallen log and made his way around it. Verdant green moss covered much of the log and he used some to rub dried blood from his hand.

He knelt and fell onto his side and then lay with his back against the log on the downhill side. The log smelled wet and rotten. He lay there breathing deeply with his feet drawn up and his arms clutching his knees.

It was growing darker and Case's hands and feet felt cold and he felt himself shivering and pressed his back tight against the moldering wood. He tried not to think about what he had seen because now he felt safe.

A long time ago in his war he had spent a night huddled behind a rotted log in a jungle and now he remembered that. In the jungle he had fought off aggressive rats through the warm night and warmth was what he needed now.

He vomited.

A nearby coyote howled and a few seconds later another answered back from somewhere far away.

Case lost consciousness.

Now he had awakened in the night and he knew he needed warmth. He needed a fire. He knew he was old and alone but decided he wanted to live.

He sat up with his back against the log and forced his right hand into his pants pocket. The pants were wet and too tight but he felt the Bird of Prey book of matches with his fingertips. It was difficult grasping the matches and pulling his hand back out of the tight pocket.

Case held the matchbook in his mouth and crawled away from the log and searched with his hands for whatever might serve as kindling. There was barely light enough from a half moon and stars to see and at first all he could find were wet leaves and ferns and a few small death-cap mushrooms. He crawled along until he came across a carpet of dry pine needles near the trunk of a tree and then some dry twigs alongside a stand of buck brush.

He piled the dry pine needles next to the buck brush and carefully crisscrossed the twigs on top and crawled back to where he had started and searched with his hands on the underside of the log for loose hunks of dry bark. He ripped off bark until he thought he had enough. It took five trips to carry the bark back to where he had piled the kindling. After the fourth trip he felt his right hand bleeding again. After the last trip to the buck brush he realized it would have taken only one trip to carry the kindling to the fuel.

"Idiot," he said to himself.

His voice sounded loud in the quiet night and his hands were so numb that he had trouble ripping a match out of the book. After he had dropped three matches trying to strike them, there were only a very few left and the fourth match scratched across the striking surface making tiny blue sparks but didn't light.

Case blew on the matches hoping to dry them out with his breath. The third match to the last struck and flared into a feeble blue and orange flame. When he lowered the match to touch it to the leaves and twigs it slipped from his fingers and fell to the wet forest floor and went out. He stuck the fingers of his right hand into his mouth. He bit the fingers and barely felt pain but after a while he thought he could hold a match. The second to last match lit when he struck it. When he carefully lowered the small flame to the kindling the dry leaves and twigs caught.

He arranged small hunks of bark carefully over the flame. It appeared the kindling flame would die and he leaned down and blew on it carefully and finally the bark caught.

"Yes," Case said and his voice sounded loud again and strange in the forest at night and he didn't speak again.

Soon he could feel warmth from the fire and he knelt close in front of the steady orange flames and held his opened hands directly over the burning bark.

He fed progressively larger pieces of bark to the fire. He knew he would be all right now and as soon as he was warmed through he would start the hike back to his cabin. Even in the dark he knew the way.

DAGWOOD AND MR. DITHERS

SUNBEAM

I n San Francisco's Haight-Ashbury district in the summer of 1967 everyone who knew her called her Sunbeam. She was seventeen years old and had hitchhiked west from Kansas City where her father presided over a prosperous bank. Her father played a lot of golf while her mother's preferred pastimes were eating lunch at expensive restaurants and shopping for clothes at exclusive stores. Traveling alone on the road west Sunbeam seldom met with anything but decent treatment. During a ride through western Kansas and Colorado she and a husky middle-aged truck driver sang folk songs for the better part of five hundred miles. Her San Francisco friends began calling her Sunbeam because she never lost her cheerful disposition in any antiwar protest or college administration building occupation or civil rights march. When cops or squares acted violently or obscenely by screaming at her or throwing eggs at her or spitting on her she responded with a benevolent smile. Sometimes she asked her tormentors to take up a banner or sign and join the parade. "Please come on along with us," she would say. "Join us! You can do it! You know you want to!" Not many wanted to and she was arrested fourteen times in two years and spent thirty-six nights in jail and never shed her smile or abandoned her positive outlook. When she was jailed during *a protest march against racial discrimination in housing she thought up a slogan that helped fuel the protest after her release:* Would you want your daughter to marry a realtor? *In 1969 she migrated north with a band of friends to form a commune in a remote mountain valley on government land. On a weekend excursion she met a boy named Drum at a hot springs pool in the woods and they soon married and soon after that they decided to grow weed, and the Bird of Prey helped launder the money they earned. After Drum died, Sunbeam kept both businesses alive. Over a period of several years she developed a product that connoisseurs believed to be equal to the finest strains of outdoor-grown cannabis found anywhere.*

On a rainy October night years ago a Ford Bronco left the Bird of Prey at closing time carrying seven deer hunters who had celebrated an eight-point buck one of them had killed, and three miles down the road the vehicle missed a curve and skidded through a guardrail and plunged into a rocky canyon. None of the men were wearing seatbelts and all seven were killed. Four were pronounced dead at the scene and three were helicoptered to the nearest hospital and soon died there.

After that accident Sunbeam began serving free half-pound buffalo burgers to anyone who wanted them at midnight. The expense was insignificant and she thought it her moral duty to do what she could to see that her customers drove home safely after she closed the tavern at 2 a.m. She knew the burgers would help counteract the beer and liquor they drank. The prime lean grass-fed buffalo was delivered every Monday afternoon and Sunbeam cooked and served the burgers herself from a small kitchen next to the back door where a counter, a walk-in cooler, and a charcoal grill stood. The burgers were served in oversized whole-wheat buns with organic lettuce and tomato and imported German mustard.

Sunbeam believed in sharing her wealth and a large white poster was nailed to the wall beside the serving counter:

BIRD OF PREY BUFFALO-BURGER CHALLENGE!!!
FINISH TEN BURGERS IN THIRTY MINUTES!!!!
WIN ONE THOUSAND DOLLARS CASH!!!!!

So far one hundred and eighty-seven customers had accepted the challenge and none had succeeded in finishing five pounds of ground buffalo meat in half an hour, but spectators always enjoyed watching people try.

A tall lean middle-aged rancher from a neighboring county had come closest. He devoured eight of the burgers in just over twenty-six minutes but then had to hurry through the tavern and out the door and into the parking lot to vomit into the bed of his pickup truck.

Tonight Shadow and Shrimp and their friend and colleague Toon sat at a table against the wall next to the serving counter with two burgers apiece and their pints of amber ale. They were saving places for Sunbeam and for two more coworkers named Shakespeare and Stones who would soon arrive.

As often happened Shadow and Shrimp were arguing about food and the restaurant they hoped to open someday soon.

"You heard that judge," Shadow said. "That dude on *Chopped* said it *twice*. Italian food's the best food there is. The *finest*! In the *world*! You *heard* it! Day before yesterday! Right? That's exactly why we got to make our place Italian."

"Yeah, I heard it, and it doesn't mean shit."

"Well why doesn't it mean shit?"

"'Cause I heard that dude's name too. Did you catch that judge's name?"

"What the fuck difference does his name make? He's a judge on *Chopped*, an expert! A fucking big-time chef!"

Shrimp swallowed beer and shook his head and smiled. "His fucking name was Antonelli. You didn't hear it? Or Antolini. Some damn name like that. The point is it ended with a goddamn *i*."

"So what?"

"So he's an Italian!"

"So what?"

"So what the fuck would you expect an Italian to say? You're Italian, right?"

"Yeah I am, part at least, but so what, that doesn't prove anything."

"It sure as shit does prove some things. You been brainwashed. I bet you grew up on spaghetti and meatballs. I bet you poured tomato sauce on your hotcakes."

"Bullshit. I'm not brainwashed. I never ate any hotcakes either."

"Listen. If that judge's name was Goldberg he'd say kosher food was the best and if he had some German name or some French name then he'd say German food or French food was the best. That's the way it is, man. That's how it goes."

Shadow swallowed a bite of buffalo burger and drank some beer. "Bullshit," he said.

"Look at it this way," Shrimp answered. "Do I look Mexican?"

"No. Do I?"

"No."

"So what the fuck?"

"Here's what the fuck. I don't look Mexican 'cause I'm *not* Mexican. But I know Mexican food is the best fucking food there is. That's because I'm objective."

"Bullshit," Shadow said again.

"Besides, there's already Italian restaurants in the area, some pizza joints too, and there's no Mexican restaurants for maybe a hundred miles. At *least* a hundred miles."

"That *is* bullshit. *Total* bullshit. There's Taco Bells practically every place you look."

"I said restaurants, dude, not shit holes."

"Italian food's popular *every*where."

"Mexican food's more popular than Italian food in America now. Do your research, then you'll learn the truth. What century you living in? Tacos are more popular than fucking hamburgers all over the country. I read a study on it."

"Who did the study?" Shadow said. "Some dude named Pancho? Who gives a shit about hamburgers? Who said hamburgers were Italian?"

"What's that you're chowing down on right now? What's that sitting right there on the table in front of you? Is it a fried chicken? A roast fucking duck?"

"It's no hamburger," Shrimp said. "It's a *buff*alo burger! Ever seen a buffalo? Does it look like a cow?"

"All I know is, the last Mexican dude I saw on *Chopped*, the last contestant I mean, he *did* look like a cow."

"That's 'cause he likes his own food. The last Italian contestant we saw on *Chopped* was the day before yesterday. Remember *that* dude? You could tell *he* couldn't eat his own cooking. He was so skinny, even his *head* was so skinny, his brain must look like a fucking waffle!"

As he ate Toon listened with little interest to Shadow and Shrimp. He didn't especially like either Italian or Mexican food and he'd heard their arguments many times before. The only thing he'd ever heard the two agree about was their plan to sneak weed into their desserts so that customers would leave the restaurant happy.

Toon had seen the television program *Chopped* once when he visited a cousin in his hometown on the Fourth of July. Four competing chefs had to prepare appetizers and main courses and desserts from "mystery baskets" of weird ingredients in a prescribed amount of time. Their efforts were tasted and judged by three well-known chefs and the winner won a $10,000 prize. Toon remembered the winner on the episode he watched because he had been a fat man with black hair and skin as white as flour who sported impressive colorful tattoos on both arms and his neck and forehead, and Toon was happy to see him take first place.

Toon had been given his name because he loved cartoons and had carefully detailed tattoos of various characters scattered over his body. On his chest was an image of Elmer Fudd with a shotgun chasing Bugs Bunny and on his back was Yosemite Sam with a pistol chasing Daffy Duck. Tom the cat chased Jerry the mouse down one thigh and Popeye chased his nemesis Bluto up the other thigh and the Coyote sprinted across his forehead on the heels of the Roadrunner whose legs were a blur. All the tattoos were expertly done and rendered in vivid color. Now that Shadow and Shrimp had finally stopped arguing over food he asked them about an idea he had been pondering for days.

"So tell me the truth," he said. "Don't shit me now. I got room on my ass for Dagwood Bumstead and Mr. Dithers. Maybe Mr. Dithers doesn't chase Dagwood all that often, but he always gives him some serious shit, right? So would they look okay? Would they fit in or be out of place?"

"If they're on your ass, who'd see them anyway?" Shadow asked.

"But I still figure maybe they'd look out of place because they're people."

"What the fuck," Shrimp said. "Yosemite Sam's a person, right? So's Elmer Fudd."

"Not *real* people though," Toon answered.

"You think Dagwood Bumstead's real?"

"He's more real than Elmer Fudd or Yosemite Sam. Or Popeye. He's got a fucking *job*."

"Popeye's got a job," Shadow said. "He's a sailor. But go ahead, get Dagwood tattooed on one cheek of your ass and Dithers on the other one. Go for it, dude."

"You really think I should?"

"Yeah, I do. I think you should. Maybe include Blondie too."

"Why Blondie?"

"Why not? She's pretty foxy. Go for it though, Blondie or not."

"I figure I might. Forget about Blondie though."

Shrimp looked across at the jukebox girl sitting at a nearby table. The huge asshole she was with looked drunker than ever. With his long black greasy hair and his black leather jacket he could have been a motorcycle gang member, and he noticed Shrimp eyeing his girl and sat up straight in his chair and stared at him and scowled.

Shrimp stared back but just then Shakespeare walked up to the table carrying two buffalo burgers in a paper-lined red plastic basket in one hand and a pint of dark English stout in the other hand. When he put the basket down and pulled out the chair between Shadow and Toon, Shrimp looked away from the motorcycle asshole to smile at Shakespeare.

"Hey, dude," he said.

"What's up?" answered Shakespeare.

Shakespeare had led a strange and nomadic life. The only traditional thing he had done as a youth was wrestle in high school and then college. At two hundred and sixty-two pounds he had been a heavyweight champion and he carried the same weight and remained solid and fit today. His name resulted from the fact that after his army discharge he proclaimed himself a writer. For more than three years now he had been working hard on a novel titled *The Adventures of Superpenis*. Like Shadow he kept his hair cut short but he wore a beard fashioned after illustrations representing William Shakespeare.

It had been Toon who suggested to Shakespeare that he model his novel's protagonist after the comic book character Plastic Man. In comic books Plastic Man's success in combating evil resulted from an ability to extend his arms and legs to any desired shapes or lengths and Superpenis could do the same thing with his penis.

"So where you been hanging, Shakespeare?" Shadow said. "What you been up to?"

"Writing," Shakespeare answered. "Ever since we got back from the woods."

"Going good?"

"Damn good, man! Somehow I do my best work when I'm tired. When I'm fuckin' wiped out in fact, like today. An' guess what? Tomorrow I got an editor calling me up. Tomorrow, man!"

"No shit?"

"No shit! I been writing letters to publishers for months and I finally got me an answer!"

"Congratulations, man. What page you on?"

"I ain't counting pages, but I bet I'm halfway through, at least. Three-quarters maybe."

"So what's ol' Superpenis up to these days?" Shrimp asked.

"Did I tell you about him busting those bank robbers along the river?"

"That happened right after he used his cock to fly-fish with, right? He tied a leader on his cock and landed a record steelhead. Sure I remember that. Yeah, you told us all about it."

Shakespeare forgot his burgers and stout and leaned forward with his arms on the tabletop to talk about his hero. "Okay, next

I got a scene set at a big cowboy rodeo going," he said. "Like one of those big ones they write about in the papers and show sometimes on TV. I had writer's fucking block all week, but I finally got it figured out today. That's why I'm late." He looked around the table to make certain all his friends were listening. "So now he's after this cowboy who's head of a gang of redneck cowboy dudes who rustle cattle and he has to get the cowboys to trust him so he shows up at this big rodeo dressed up in western clothes and he enters the calf-roping contest. You know calf roping, right? When they ride on a horse after a calf and they got to lasso the calf and jump off the horse and flip the calf over and tie his legs up. So Superpenis wears baggy pants and a baggy shirt so nobody in the crowd can tell he's using his penis as his lasso. He uses his penis to lasso the calf and his penis-lasso drags the calf right back to him while he's jumping off his horse. Then he uses his penis-rope to tie the calf up and he breaks the world calf-roping record. Some cowboys get pissed off at him winning the prize money, and other cowboys think he's cool. *Most* cowboys think he's cool. He gets in tight with the ones who think he's cool. So he'll go on from there to figure out about the cattle rustling. Then he'll figure out how the rustling is part of this huge crime syndicate in Chicago. Chicago's where the slaughterhouses are where the rustlers sell the cattle. By the time he gets to Chicago I'll figure out another cool way he can use his penis there."

"I still think you should call the dude Supercock," Shrimp said.

"I told you about ten times. *Twenty* times. Cock's too crude. This is a sophisticated novel. Subtle even."

Shakespeare finally took a swallow of his stout and leaned back in his chair and looked around the table expectantly. Shadow and Toon smiled at him and Shrimp looked down at the table and shook his head. "Sophisticated my ass," he said.

As all four men began eating and drinking Stones arrived with his burgers and his pint of pilsner and took one of the two remaining chairs. Stones was bearded and long-haired like Shrimp and wore baggy jeans and a blue and gold sweatshirt. He had been a defensive end in high school and college and when he couldn't make the NFL he joined the army and fought and lost his right eye. After the army he failed at professional wrestling and various other short-lived jobs. Now he wore stylish patches to cover the empty eye socket. He owned a collection of patches that came in various colors and patterns including a bloodshot eye on a black patch for the rare occasions he suffered hangovers. Tonight he wore a Scottish plaid patch in bright red and lime green. "Sorry I'm late," Stones said. "I've been traveling. The lot's so crowded I had to park out on the road. I'm hungry." He bit into a burger and chewed and swallowed and drank some pilsner and took another big bite of his burger.

Everybody went to work on the burgers. They all knew that Stones had been spending a lot of time on the road lately but nobody knew why and Stones didn't want them to know. His life had begun to change six weeks back on a Saturday afternoon when he had been driving to the nearest town where he could purchase job supplies. That day he had planned to buy extra-tough work gloves and a flex-tine harrow and a new brush hoe. The town was one hundred eleven miles from

Stones's cabin, and eight miles out of town he picked up a hitchhiker.

The hitchhiker jogged along the side of the road to the Subaru and opened the back door and tossed in his backpack. He was wearing Jesus sandals and dressed in threadbare jeans and a sweat-stained white T-shirt and a dirty green baseball cap. "Thanks, man," he said to Stones. "I sure do appreciate it, dude."

"Climb on in," Stones said.

The hitchhiker slammed the back door and opened the front door and climbed in.

"Where you headed?" Stones asked him.

"The homeless shelter, man."

"In town?"

"Yeah, in town. They got one now. It's new."

"So you're homeless then?"

"Sure as shit am. They even got showers there at the shelter. They got a food bank too. They got this cute little girl works there most days. Prettiest little thing you ever saw. She puts in some *hours*, man. I mean she hangs out there morning, noon, and night. So I can get myself cleaned up and grab some eats. I could even stay there if I wanted. Overnight I mean. But I dig the woods. I got my tent set up by a nice clean spring. I got my Coleman lantern, my propane stove, my fire pit, a nice smooth log to plant my ass on. I dig my camp."

As he drove toward town Stones glanced at his passenger. It was hard to guess his age. He was pale and skinny and there were streaks of gray in the long brown hair that stuck out from under his cap and in his thick brown beard.

"That a dog tag you got hangin' on your car keys there?" the homeless man asked.

"Yep."

"Don't mind me asking you, man, but is the army what happened to your eye? Combat?"

"Right again."

"I threw my fucking dog tags away when I got out. I never even got wounded but I tossed 'em in a fuckin' dumpster."

"I understand that," Stones said. "Where abouts is the homeless shelter? I never knew there was one."

"Out by the grange. There's this old gas station that closed down and they made it into a homeless shelter. It's right out there past the grange. Half a mile. You know where the grange is?"

"Oh yeah. That's where I'm headed. The grange."

"Cool!"

Stones drove past the grange to the homeless shelter and parked. The only other car out front was a Dodge Dart. He remembered when the building had been a gas station. Now the old place had been freshly painted bright green. "Here," Stones said and he handed the homeless man a $50 bill.

"Hey, man. You kiddin' me? Is this motherfucker genuine? Is it real?"

"Oh yeah, it's real."

"Thanks, man! I mean *thanks*!"

"No *problema*," Stones answered. "I guess since I'm here I'll take a look inside."

The homeless man retrieved his pack from the backseat and Stones followed him into the building.

The first thing Stones saw was the small girl sitting behind a wooden desk. On the desk were a telephone and a computer and a small stack of papers anchored by a round river stone serving as a paperweight. Directly behind the desk were long shelves of canned and packaged foods reaching from the floor to the ceiling. Stones looked at the little girl and liked her at once and knew he wanted to help her. He wanted to be near her and he wanted to protect her if he ever could.

"Hello, Lan," the hitchhiker said.

"Hello," the girl answered. "Welcome!"

She had shiny black hair and smooth brown Asian features and when she looked at Stones he saw she was frightened of him and he knew it had to be his size that made her afraid. After a quick calculation he figured he outweighed her by at least a hundred and fifty pounds.

When the hitchhiker went off to shower in a back room Stones offered to help Lan. He told her he had time to spare and if anything needed doing around the place he'd be happy to do it. At first she shook her head no, but he saw the cardboard boxes of food goods on the floor behind her desk and he offered to unload the boxes and stack the goods on the shelves. She looked at him with fear in her eyes but finally nodded her head yes and he ripped open boxes and began shelving canned goods and cartons of noodles and bags of rice.

Neither of them spoke while he worked.

The phone rang once and Lan gave someone directions to the shelter.

When the hitchhiker came back showered and dressed he helped Stones finish stocking the shelves.

After they were done Stones shook hands with the hitchhiker. "You need a ride back to your camp?" he asked him. "I'll be headed back after the grange."

"No thanks, man. I got to use the computer here." He nodded at the desk and Lan smiled. "Got to email my brother down south. The dude worries about me. Need some hot coffee too. They got good coffee back there by the shower room."

"Good luck," Stones said.

"Thanks again, dude! You're a good man!"

"Good-bye, Lan," Stones said. "I'll come by whenever I'm in town to see if you need any help."

She nodded again from behind the desk but didn't answer and Stones could see she was still afraid.

"That man's so *big*," he heard Lan say when he was out the door.

In the six weeks since he had first seen her Stones had been back to the homeless shelter twenty-eight times. The first time she had seen him and been afraid Stones had been wearing loose-fitting khaki pants and a baggy light gray sweatshirt and he felt that light-colored clothing made him look even bigger than he was. He remembered how white uniforms always made football players look bigger so now he always wore dark tight-fitting clothes to the shelter.

He had unloaded and stacked more food. He had swept and mopped the place. He had sanded and painted old furniture. He had laundered sheets and towels and he had twice done work on Lan's old Dodge Dart.

Gradually Lan overcame her fear and the two of them had brief conversations as Stones worked. Lan came from Oakland and had majored in sociology and graduated from Cal-Berkeley and now lived in town with a cousin who owned a café. The shelter was funded by a nonprofit and she earned little money but believed in her chosen vocation. They had been open for only two months and few of the homeless came for help but more came all the time as word spread. Stones told Lan that he worked on an organic farm and believed in his vocation too. He never told her anything about his past and he never spoke of her to anybody else.

For Stones the strangest thing about their relationship was the fact that no matter how often he saw Lan he could never remember what she looked like. When he talked to her his pulse raced and he studied her face. He loved her lustrous hair and her bright dark eyes and her high cheekbones and her perfectly formed nose and her smooth and flawless skin. But once she was gone from his sight he found it impossible to picture her face in his mind. Today Lan had worked the evening shift and Stones drove in after the trouble in the woods and spent an hour sanding down old donated wooden chairs and talking to her. When he said good-bye she surprised and delighted him. She walked with him out to his Subaru and shook his big hand. It was the first time they had touched.

"I'll make it back tomorrow morning," Stones said, "to finish up those chairs. Good night, Lan."

Instead of merely saying "Good night" she smiled up and said, "Stones, I like you very much."

At the crowded table in the Bird of Prey Stones tried hard to create an image of Lan's smiling face in his mind and now it worked and he could see her clearly.

"Hey, Stones, what the hell you smiling about?" Shakespeare said.

"Nothing special," Stones answered without looking up from his burger.

"Yeah, well right before you got here I was telling these dudes more about Superpenis. You want to hear about him too? You want to get caught up?"

"I guess so," Stones said. "Why not?"

But before Shakespeare could begin repeating his rodeo scene Sunbeam stepped up to the table.

She was sixty-four years old and anyone who saw her could easily tell she had been a true beauty. She had perfect teeth and short white hair that was always neatly combed framing green eyes and high cheekbones. Tonight she wore beige slacks and a black silk blouse. She was tall and tanned and slim and erect and stood behind the last remaining vacant chair smiling at the five young men she thought of as her foot soldiers.

"There's a welcome break at the burger counter," she told them as she took her seat. "A short break though. But I at least have time to say hello."

All the men nodded at her and smiled politely.

"At least we can get started," she said. "I got some news from Deputy Winter this afternoon. He stopped in for a margarita."

"Winter," Shadow said. "If you ask me he's an unreliable news source."

"No time for euphemisms now," Sunbeam said. "'Unreliable news source my ass. Call it what it is. He's a fat ugly shit-kicker. But for better or worse he's the source we have at hand and he wanted to tell me he's heard about a gang of scumbags from somewhere down south who want to rip us off right before we harvest."

"Maybe that's it," Shadow said. "If he's right it makes sense. We caught some scumbags this afternoon out by the grow by Piston Rock. We kicked their sorry asses."

"How many?"

"Three is all. Or four. I thought I saw an old dude out ahead of the three we got, but we never found him."

"We looked all over," Shrimp said, "but we couldn't find anybody."

"We tried," said Shakespeare. "We worked at it hard. But that's some thick woods and tough country out there."

"Don't start fretting yet," Sunbeam said. "Winter promised he'd keep me informed."

"But like you say yourself he's a fat shit and a stupid asshole," Toon said. "I mean you said it right, he is. I wouldn't piss on Winter if he caught fire. How'd he find out anyway? How's he know? Where's the sheriff stand in this?"

"Never mind the sheriff," Sunbeam said. "The sheriff himself's definitely and obviously yet another scumbag. You're right about Winter, he's a certified dumb ass, and it's a good thing he is. Good for us I mean. I told you what I heard. I need to head on back to the counter now. Some guy, some stranger, wants to try the challenge. Just found out a few minutes ago."

"The burgers?" Shrimp asked.

"What else?" Sunbeam answered.

"What stranger?" asked Toon.

"A fat man in a weird camouflage cowboy hat with a rattle-snake hatband. He wants his burgers at midnight on the dot."

"That dude," Stones said. "He's weird for sure. Why midnight?"

"How would I know?" Sunbeam said. "I didn't ask him. Maybe he's superstitious. We'll talk more later, men. See you soon."

Sunbeam went back behind the counter to prepare ten half-pound buffalo burgers for the fat cowboy in the camouflage hat.

With many patrons sitting with their buffalo burgers in front of them the Bird of Prey had turned fairly quiet with at least as much eating as talking or drinking going on.

"If I Said You Had a Beautiful Body Would You Hold It Against Me?" by the Bellamy Brothers played on the jukebox. Six couples slow-danced to the song on the small hardwood floor between the bar and the crowded tables.

Shrimp sat eyeing the motorcycle dude and the sexy blond again. She was holding her beautiful body close against him when Sunbeam carried the platter of ten oversized burgers out from behind the counter. She carried the platter with both hands through the crowd toward a table near the bar where the fat cowboy sat waiting.

Word spread quickly and nearly everyone in the place including the dancers gathered into a crowd around the table to watch.

Sunbeam carefully lowered the platter and placed it in front of the cowboy and stood up straight and looked at her wristwatch. "Two minutes till midnight," she announced in a loud voice.

"I need me two big pitchers of water," the cowboy said.

"Two pitchers of water please!" Sunbeam called to Rainbow.

"Make it quick!" said the cowboy.

Rainbow hurried out from behind the bar and placed a two-quart pitcher filled with water and ice on each side of the burger platter.

"Want a glass?" Sunbeam asked.

"I'll down it straight from the pitcher," the cowboy said. "Saves time."

"Ready?" Sunbeam asked.

The fat cowboy lifted his hat from his head and set it on the table behind the burger platter. He had long, brown greasy hair with a white bald spot in the middle. He took three deep breaths and massaged his jaw muscles with both hands and smiled and nodded.

"Good luck," Sunbeam said. "Coming up on midnight... *Go!*"

The hatless cowboy lifted the first burger with both hands and took a huge bite and chewed hard and fast and swallowed and took another huge bite and chewed and swallowed and then lifted a water pitcher with one hand and drank deeply from it and swallowed twice and lowered the pitcher back to the table and bit into his burger again with water dribbling down his chin onto his neck. He finished the first burger in less than two minutes. Smears of shiny grease mixed with yellow mustard were visible around his mouth as he lifted the second burger and bit in and chewed and swallowed and drank again.

Except for occasional shouts of encouragement the crowd watched in deferential silence.

"Do it dude!" someone yelled.

"Go dude!"

"Grind, baby! Grind!"

"Yeah! You the man!"

"Eat it, dude! Go! Go! Go!"

In fourteen minutes five burgers were gone along with one pitcher of water. The fat cowboy's face had gone as pale as his bald spot, but he picked up the sixth burger and just as he bit into it the front door flew open.

Two big men wearing jeans and black leather jackets with their faces covered with bright red ski masks that revealed only their eyes and their mouths burst into the tavern closely followed by six more identically dressed men who pushed through the open door in pairs. By the time all the intruders were inside the brawl was under way.

No one in the crowd noticed that the fat cowboy spat a mouthful of burger onto the floor and clamped his hat on his head as he rose from the table and quickly circled the gang of intruders and disappeared out the door into the night.

The first two masked men were punching and kicking the first men they had come to once inside.

Women screamed and some of them ran behind the bar and others into the restroom as men screamed and cursed.

"Motherfucker!"

"Cocksucker!"

"Fuck you!"

"Suck that, faggot!"

"Fuck you!"

"I'll rip your lungs out, motherfucker!"

"Fuck you!"

Rainbow had run behind the bar and ducked down to call Deputy Winter on the landline.

Sunbeam made it back behind her serving counter.

Shadow and Shrimp and Toon and Shakespeare and Stones were joined in the battle.

Somewhere near the bar a shot was fired.

"Motherfucker!"

"Fuck you motherfucker!"

"Faggot!"

Another shot was fired as Stones came up behind one of the masked men and grabbed the shoulder of his jacket with his left hand and spun him around and landed a hard, solid punch to the Adam's apple with his right. The man clutched his throat with both hands and made a loud ugly gurgling noise as he fell.

Another masked man had the motorcycle dude who had been dancing with the blond backed against the bar landing one hard blow to the face after another. As the motorcycle dude fell backward onto the bar Shadow saw the gashed cheek and closed eye and swollen ear, and he brought his boot up with all his might between the masked man's legs from behind. Shadow felt his boot flatten balls and the masked man grunted and screamed and spun around and crumpled to the floor. He landed curled up on his side and rocked back and forth with his eyes squeezed shut and his mouth contorted with pain. Then as Shadow kicked the red mask with the toe of his boot where he knew the nose should be, something smashed into his skull and just as he felt himself begin to fall everything went black.

STONES

As early as kindergarten Stones had been big for his age so he had always played football. From the very start he was so good at the game that beginning in elementary school his teachers forgave his laziness and irresponsibility. No matter how poor his work was he was given passing grades all the way through high school and three years of college. No one including Stones cared about his grades beyond the academic requirement that minimal standards had to be met to keep him eligible to play. Stones believed along with his parents and coaches and friends that after Saturday football at a major college he would play on Sundays in the NFL. But he didn't quite make it. He was big enough and fast enough and athletic enough but he wasn't quite mean enough. "You don't enjoy *hurting people!" a coach admonished him not long before he was cut. "You got to love dishing out pain!" After the army at age twenty-three and minus his right eye he found his way to professional wrestling. He began his career as a villain dubbed Pirate Pete and he grew a beard and entered the ring with a bright red bandanna wrapped around his head and carrying a shiny broadsword to go along with his eye patch. The problem was he sometimes forgot his instructions and managed to lose matches he was scripted to win. Next he was hired as a bouncer in a nightclub but after a few weeks on that job he shoved an obnoxious drunk down the steep flight of stairs that led from the street up to club and the drunk collided with a middle-aged couple starting up the stairs and knocked them all the way out the door and across the sidewalk onto the street. The man was struck by a car and nearly died and Stones was fired and a lawsuit was filed against the nightclub. Thanks to family connections, the police department in a coastal town trained Stones despite his missing eye and took him on as a probationary beat patrolman. On a cloudy evening a few weeks after starting work he set out on foot down a lonely beach chasing two men who had just robbed a 7-Eleven at knifepoint. He caught up with one of the robbers and handcuffed him with his arms stretched backward around a palm tree and then set off running again and eventually caught the second robber farther down the beach and took him straight back to the station to be booked. He forgot about the palm tree man who wasn't discovered until late the next morning and this resulted in a lawsuit filed against the town and Stones was fired again, but one of his friends on the force had told him about the money to be made up north in marijuana country.*

THAT POOR SUMBITCH

Case reached his cabin shortly before 3 a.m.

He stripped and stood sick and exhausted under a strong hot shower for half an hour. After the shower he wrapped himself in a terrycloth robe and then arranged crumpled newsprint with kindling and small chunks of madrone in his woodstove and lit a fire.

Next he made a thick ham sandwich with horseradish on dark rye bread.

When the sandwich was gone he poured three inches of Jack Daniels into a clean tumbler and pulled his favorite rocking chair up close to the stove and sat there sipping the bourbon and warming himself through. With the fire burning steadily he added larger chunks of the well-seasoned madrone and soon the woodstove roared with emanating heat. Case's legs were stiff and sore and his right shoulder ached badly. The old wound on his back itched and the itching irritated him more than the various pains.

He limped to the kitchen for ingredients and rolled a healthy joint and limped back and smoked it by the woodstove, and it helped.

When the joint was gone he thought mostly of Heather for the half hour it took to finish the tumbler of Jack Daniels. She had been dead for more than eight years and the long days and lonely nights and tiresome months had passed too slowly ever since he had been living alone.

After the last sip of bourbon he stoked the fire and carried the tumbler out to the kitchen and filled it with water and swallowed three Advil tablets and placed the empty glass on top of the sandwich plate in the sink. Then he climbed the stairs to his loft and set his alarm for 8 a.m. He dropped the robe over a chair and slid into bed and fell asleep almost at once and dreamed of Heather.

The alarm awakened Case and he showered under warm water and brushed and flossed his teeth and shaved. He had come to dislike these basic daily rituals because they brought to mind better times when he wasn't alone and had more reason to care about his hygiene and appearance.

In his bedroom he dressed in jeans and a heavy woolen sweater and then phoned the Sheriff's Office. Deputy Winter answered in a sleepy drawling voice. Case told him what he had seen in the woods the previous afternoon and Winter told Case he'd be out to his place within the hour to talk about it.

Case's aches and pains had subsided. He started a pot of coffee and made another thick ham sandwich for breakfast and rebuilt the fire in the woodstove with kindling and madrone. By the time the fire was burning well the coffee was ready. He carried a mug sweetened with sugar to the rocking chair beside the stove and sat in the comforting heat.

He thought about Heather again. He couldn't help himself if he tried and he didn't want to try. He liked remembering the best times of their life together. They had lived here in this cabin in the woods since two years after Case returned from war. The Forest Service had given Case his old job back after his convalescence and he held it and did it well enough until he retired. The best thing about retirement was the mornings. After they woke up at dawn Case and Heather stayed in bed and listened to Steller's jays and robins in the trees outside the open bedroom window. They listened to the birds and talked and gazed at each other and each saw love in the other's eyes. Sometimes they made love.

Sitting close to the fire with his coffee Case remembered the October morning with Heather when low-flying flocks of Canada geese migrating south had passed close and steadily over the cabin roof for half an hour.

He added madrone to the woodstove and replenished his coffee. When he heard Winter's jeep winding up the gravel road he was glad. He didn't like Winter but now the solitude would end for a while. He poured more coffee and added sugar and carried the mug out onto the deck to meet the deputy.

The deck caught early sunlight through a break in the tall trees and the sun's warmth worked against the chill of morning.

Winter stopped the jeep a few feet from the steep flight of steps that led up to the deck. He pulled the handbrake and opened the door and climbed out waving at Case. Then he stood beside his vehicle and yawned and stretched. He was a short fat man with a thick black mustache and a round white face with a nose as red as a cherry.

"Hey there, Case," he said.

Case was an outsider but even he had learned that Winter hated his childhood nickname. "Hello, Hog," he said.

Winter looked at him. "So how's it goin'?" he said.

"Not so shabby. How's it going with you? Come on up."

"The world's gone nuts, that's how."

"It's been nuts a long time," Case answered. "Before we ever got here."

"Well, yeah, hell yes, but it's gettin' worse. Jesus, you sure you made these steps steep enough?"

"I think I did. Come on inside."

"Hell, let's talk out here. It's nice. I'm stuck inside all day mostly."

Winter had winded himself climbing the steps.

"Coffee?" Case asked him.

"Hell yes."

"Cream? Sugar?"

"Both."

"Be right back."

"Thanks, Case."

"You're welcome, Hog."

Case left his mug on the deck railing and went into the cabin and soon returned with a mug of coffee for Winter who tasted it and smacked his lips and smiled. "That's some good shit!" he said.

"Glad you like it."

It always took Winter a long time to get to the point in a conversation. "Hear about ol' Butler?" he asked. "About that big ol' buck he drilled?"

"No," Case answered. "Where?"

"Out on Holtzhauer's spread. He trespassed an' ol' Holtzhauer was pissed! He called me out to arrest ol' Butler. Turns out Holtzhauer had his eye on that same buck. That buck was one big sumbitch!"

Case drank from his own coffee and looked at Winter who was still breathing hard from his climb. Steam rose from Winter's mug and he lifted the mug up close to his bulbous red nose to inhale the aroma. "Smells mighty good!" he said. "This here is some good shit!"

"What'd you do to Butler? Anything?"

"Ol' Holtzhauer thinks he's King Shit when it comes to his land. Hell, it was his great-granddaddy got all that land in the first place way back when property around here was damn near free. Holtzhauer didn't do jack shit to get that property, but he thinks he's King Shit on it now."

Case watched a Steller's jay land on the lower limb of a nearby Douglas fir. The jay's head bobbed up and down as he scolded. Another jay landed on the same limb and joined in. "What'd you do to Butler?" he asked Winter.

"Ol' Holtzhauer calls me once a week, sometimes twice a week, sometimes *three* goddamn times a week to tell me how the potheads grow their shit, their weed, somewhere down there south of his big red barn. Down there by Pass Creek."

"Do they grow down there?"

"I been down there a time or two. Nosed around pretty good. Never saw one damn thing about any growing."

"I think the people I saw yesterday might have been growers. Or might have been ripping off the local growers. Or might have been both."

"This coffee's some good shit! What kind is it?"

"I think it's called Coastal's Best. All I do is buy whatever's on sale."

"That's smart! That Holtzhauer's got more deer on his property than anybody could count, and elk too in wintertime, once it snows. That land he got is like a deer an' elk farm. A preserve! So what's his problem? That's what I wonder."

"What happened about Butler?"

"I talked to him some. Gave him some friendly advice about where he should shoot his buck next time. I guess he liked what I said 'cause he gave me some venison steaks. What I say is, fuck Holtzhauer. Pardon my French. You like Holtzhauer?"

"I barely know him," Case said. "We travel in different circles."

"Well you may not know him but you know about 'im. Draft dodger. You know *that* much. He's pretty near my age an' he sure as shit never served his country. *Our* country. His old man pulled some strings. I heard all about *that*. That's why I say fuck 'im. You an' me went. You an' me almos' got our asses shot off."

Both men drank some coffee. With the sun higher in the sky the morning was warming quickly. Case noticed that the jays were gone from the tree limb. Directly overhead he saw the long north-to-south line of a jet trail stretching across the blue sky.

"Butler give me ten, twelve pounds off that buck. You like venison?"

"I like elk better."

"Hell, most everybody likes elk better. You like venison though?"

"Sure, I like it well enough."

"You like salmon?"

"I like salmon. But I like steelhead better."

"I like salmon better. This coffee's some good shit! I went duck huntin' day before yesterday. I almost asked you if you liked duck. Reason I didn't ask is, I figured you'd say you like pheasant better. Tell me, you got many bats out here?"

"Bats?"

"Yeah, bats. Mice with wings. I got 'em in my house sometimes. Flyin' around at night right inside my bedroom. Finally figured out how to deal with 'em. I swat those little fuckers with a tennis racket. They don't bleed after you swat 'em that way so it works out good. You got many?"

"Not inside," Case said. "Sometimes they're all over the place outside here after sunset."

"You're a lucky man. How often you go into town to shop?"

"Every couple weeks."

"It's a long drive. Next time I go, I'm buyin' some a this Coastal's Best. This is some damn good shit! You hear what happened at the tavern last night?"

"The Bird of Prey? No, what?"

"I mean, what the hell, there ain't any other taverns around here for forty, fifty miles, at least that far, right? They had a brawl is what. Late at night, after Sunbeam started serving her buffalo burgers. You go to the Bird of Prey much? I seen you there once or twice."

"I stop in for beers in the daytime. Not often though and I've never been there at night. I like Sunbeam though. I like Rainbow a lot. I visit her husband Uncle Sam sometimes in the afternoon.

Heather used to help with Uncle Sam. She and Rainbow were friends. It seems like a good tavern. You got anything against it?"

"Me? Hell no. It's a damn good place. Fine beer, fine whiskey, fine burgers too. It's a sad thing about ol' Uncle Sam. That poor sumbitch. But I guess he did his duty, right? I guess he did it like lots of us did! The government ought to take better care of 'im though. Pardon my French again, but I can't help it, sometimes what I say is, fuck the government!"

"We both worked for the government though. You still do."

"I got me three more years is all. Thirty-seven months is all. That's all she wrote! After that, fishin' an' huntin'!"

"More coffee?"

"I could stand some. It's some real good shit."

"I'll get us both some."

Case took the empty mugs back into the cabin. He didn't mind the way Winter talked without saying much or getting anywhere because it passed the time. Having Winter around was slightly better than having nobody. But today Winter seemed somehow ill at ease. He seemed stiff and had a guilty or nervous look in his eyes and seemed to be hiding something, and Case couldn't imagine what it might be.

When Case poured the mugs full it nearly emptied the pot. He turned off the heat under the pot and walked back outside where Winter reached for his mug with a wide smile on his fat face. "This coffee, this Coastal's Best, is some good shit!" he said. "That brawl I tol' you about? Started off while some guy was goin' after ten burgers. You know, that challenge Sunbeam has. That's what she calls it, a challenge. Might try it myself sometime. Ten buffalo burgers in half an hour? I maybe could do that! I could sure as shit try! I do like buffalo! Anyway, some scumbags from someplace else marched into the Bird of Prey late las' night an' started punchin' and kickin' and cussin' and makin' threats. No provocation! No *nothin'*! The way I figure, it couldn't've been the Big Dude from across the mountain. What I heard is, the Big Dude and Sunbeam got a truce. Well, whoever the hell it was, they damn sure got what they deserved. Those boys, those vets that hang out there with Sunbeam, they know how to punch an' kick too. Kick *ass* is what I'm sayin'. That big sumbitch they call Stones? That one-eyed boy kicked some *serious* ass! After maybe two, three minutes those strangers hustled right back out the front door as fast as they come in to start with. *Faster* maybe. One or two got *carried* out. Carried out or dragged. 'Course I wasn't there, I heard about it is all, but I heard from Sunbeam herself an' from the vet crowd. You know those vet boys?"

"No I don't. Not really. When I go to the Bird of Prey it's in the afternoon. From what I hear the vets hang out there at night."

Winters swallowed more coffee and then placed his mug on the railing. Then he put one hand on the railing and shaded his eyes with the other hand and leaned forward. Case saw that on the thick little finger of the hand on the railing Winter wore a gold ring with a dark blue sapphire setting that glinted in the sunlight.

"I thought I saw a quail over there by that manzanita," Winter said. "You got quail that close?"

"There's a covey of mountain quail around, a big covey in fact. At least twenty birds."

Winter picked up his mug from the railing. "Mountain quail?" he said. "You hunt 'em?"

"No," Case said, "I don't."

"So it's true what I heard, you gave up huntin'?"

"It's true."

"How come?"

"I don't feel good about shooting anything anymore."

"How come?"

"I just don't."

"No offense, Case, but if it was me, an' I know it *ain't* me, I'd ground-sluice those little fuckers ever' chance I got. They make some damn good eatin'."

"What about those strangers? Where'd they come from and where'd they go? Did you lock them up or not?"

"You told me you like pheasant. Well how the hell do you get any pheasants if you quit huntin'?"

"I didn't say I liked pheasants. You said you figured I did. Remember?"

"You didn't say you like pheasant?"

"No."

"You still fish?"

"I still fish."

"Well how come you kill fish if you don't like killin' birds?"

"I release what I catch, except for hatchery fish. I kill them."

"How come?"

"They don't belong in the river. They pollute the native gene pool. I think I'm doing the river a favor by taking them out."

"Gene pool?"

"Gene pool."

"I see you got a big satellite dish up there. You watch lots of TV? You see that Panthers game two nights ago?"

"I never watch till the playoffs start."

"You watch bass fishin' ever?"

"No," Case said. "Do you?"

"Hell no! I got no reason to watch that shit!"

"How come you asked me if I watched?"

"I got no reason *not* to ask. You know the one they call Shadow?"

"I know about him. Maybe I've seen him around once or twice. Those boys hang out at the tavern at night."

"Well that brawl didn't work out exactly right for Shadow. This is all hearsay but I hear he kicked some ass too but then he got coldcocked from behind. Nobody saw what happened exactly but there he was, flat on his face on the floor after his buddies chased those scumbags out the door."

"Is he okay?"

"Hey! Look! There's that quail again! That's a valley quail I saw, not mountain."

"You certain?"

"I guess I know me a valley quail from a mountain quail. Hell, it ain't much harder than knowin' a pintail duck from a Canada goose. Ever shot a gadwall?"

"I don't think I ever saw one. I'm not sure I ever even heard of one."

"The only one I ever saw's the one I shot. Me an' Rufus was over on Marsh Lake one opening day a long time back. A duck flew over early, hardly light yet, *wasn't* light yet in fact, an' we both blasted away an' let that duck have it an' down he came. My dog Shorty retrieved that bird in the dark. We didn't know what the hell kind it was. Rufus thought he shot it but I knew I did. Rufus looked it up in a book later an' told me it was a gadwall. Looked kind of like a mallard hen but it was bigger. It was a goddamn gadwall. At least Rufus claimed it was. You remember my dog Shorty?"

"The yellow lab?"

"That's the one! Well, anyway, Case, what I'm thinkin' is what you saw out in the woods might have somethin' to do with what happened at the Bird of Prey. It's only a theory but it makes sense to me. You know it's damn near harvest time around here now. Hell, everybody knows that. Pot's growin' everywhere you look. Who cares? But we can't have strangers messin' around with it in these parts. We all got a good, quiet life here. You know what I mean? Yeah, you know. Don't you know?"

"Sure, I know what you mean."

"Who knows who's growin' it? Who cares? I mean, they grow on federal land, an' you can't find it all. No matter how much you find there's a hell of a lot more you don't find and not one damn plant belongs to anybody. Not *legally* it don't. With all this federal land around here, who'd be dumb enough to grow pot on his *own* land? Not even Holtzhauer that dumb. Fuck Holtzhauer that's what I say. So why bother with it? I got to fill out a report is all. Got to have the paperwork all filled out and filed away. Got to make everything official. We got to keep the strangers out is all. Know what I mean?"

Case smiled and nodded at Winter. "I sure do," he said.

Winter set his empty mug back on the deck railing and smiled and reached out to shake hands with Case. "Time for me to put some wheels on the whorehouse," he said.

"To do what?"

"Haul ass! Thanks for talkin'." Winter turned and made his way slowly down the steps with one hand on the staircase railing all the way. After he climbed into the jeep he turned his head to look up at Case and smile again. "What's that coffee called again?" he asked.

"Coastal's Best."

"Next time in town I'm gonna purchase me some!"

Winter started up the jeep and backed slowly up and then leaned out the window and called back at Case: "You rest easy now, Case!"

"What?"

"I said rest easy!"

"What's that mean?"

"Take it easy! Relax! Things'll be fine!"

Winter's head disappeared and the jeep lurched forward and rolled away.

WINTER

His great-great-great-grandparents Caleb and Myrtle Winter had come to this country as newly married pioneers. As years passed Caleb impregnated Myrtle fourteen times and eight boys and three girls survived. From the start the Winter family farmed more than three

hundred acres of prime land and that land had remained in the fam-
ily until Deputy Winter's father Orville took the advice of a friend
and began playing the stock market. In five months all the family's
money and land was gone. The day after the last twenty acres had
been sold off, Orville drank a bottle of whiskey and carefully drove
to the Bird of Prey where he knew he would find the friend who
had touted the stock market sitting at the bar drinking beer and
eating salted peanuts. Orville walked into the tavern carrying an old
double-barreled twelve-gauge Ithaca shotgun with two triggers. The
trigger in front fired the modified-choke barrel and the rear trigger
fired the full-choke barrel, and Orville walked straight up to the bar
and pulled both triggers at once and blew his friend's head off. At the
murder trial Orville entered a guilty plea and was sentenced to life
in prison without the possibility of parole and his son became a law
enforcement officer before the year was out.

BACHUS BOOKS

CHARITY

She was born to an unwed teenage mother and adopted by a childless couple who both taught elementary school in a mid-sized Midwestern town. They raised her with love but when she was nine the adoptive parents died in a plane crash and her paternal aunt was the only family member left alive to take her. The aunt was a heavy drinker and couldn't hold a job. She and Charity soon began moving from town to town and state to state. In a succession of elementary and middle schools Charity grew up homely and skinny and gawky and at school was either bullied or ignored. Then from age fourteen to sixteen she found herself transformed into a striking young woman who turned heads wherever she went. While this was happening her aunt's drinking grew worse and after she lost a part-time job as a salesperson in a hardware store she remained unemployed for more than a year. She collected welfare and food stamps and used food banks and stayed home in their dingy little apartment and drank cheap booze sitting at the kitchen table or went out to drink in cheap neighborhood bars. Whenever Charity was home she cared for her aunt and cleaned up after her as best she could. Late one summer afternoon her aunt came home gaunt and disheveled from a nearby bar with a pink-faced fat man wearing a

*baggy suit and a gaudy tie. The fat man stared at Charity and her
aunt took her into the kitchen and told her if she would go into the
bedroom with the stranger he would pay them five hundred dollars
in cash and then they could afford another month's rent and some
groceries. Charity walked out of the kitchen and through the living
room without looking at the fat man sitting on the couch and she
kept going out the front door and never came back and she never saw
her aunt again and had no idea what became of her and didn't care.*

When Shadow regained consciousness it was past nine o'clock
in the morning. He was afraid to open his eyes because he wasn't
certain whether he was dead or alive, and if he was dead he
had to be in a strange new place and he didn't want to find out
what it was like there. He was afraid to know. The same thing
had happened to him three times in war. Roadside blasts had
burned him and ruptured his eardrums and knocked him cold
for hours. The last time it happened he had remained uncon-
scious for two days.

He had never believed in the heaven his father preached about
and after all he'd seen at war he became more certain than ever
that people didn't deserve heaven anyway. Many of the dead and
mutilated had been his friends. But he didn't want to believe that
eternal oblivion was the only possible end and he couldn't imagine what else there could be and even if there was something else
he could find no logical reason to think it might be better than
what he had known before. So now in the morning he lay flat on
his back with his eyes squeezed tightly shut and a bitter taste in

his mouth and his head pounding horribly and afraid to think or move or try to talk or open his eyes.

"Are you awake? You're awake, aren't you?"

It was Charity's voice so he knew he was alive and knew where he was so he opened his eyes and there she was looking down at him and looking as frightened as he had been when he awakened.

"Good morning," she said. She tried to smile.

He wasn't sure he could talk so he made himself smile back.

"Can you hear me?"

He nodded slightly.

"But you can't talk?"

He shook his head.

"Somebody smashed you from behind on the head with a bottle. A *full* bottle. Toon saw it happen and Shakespeare and Shrimp saw the guy who did it running out the door right afterwards. Shrimp drove you to Doc's and he stitched you up. Twenty-three stitches. He had to shave all the hair off the back of your head. It looks kind of like a football back there. Or a baseball. He shot you up with some kind of painkiller. It'll work till about lunchtime. After that it might start to hurt. You have to go back in to see Doc in three days. He said you should just rest up today."

While Charity told Shadow what had happened she looked straight into his eyes and he looked straight back at her with his head gradually clearing as she talked. He could tell she was truly sorry and cared about him. He had known that already but seeing it now allowed him to feel a faint happiness along with his pain and rage. Her long blond hair had been washed and he smelled the shampoo. Her teeth were straight and white and she wore no lipstick. Most of the buttons of her loose blue blouse were undone and she never wore a bra because she didn't need one so he could see her tanned breasts and her dark nipples. When she bent down to kiss his forehead her breasts disappeared.

His arms were on top of the blanket and when Charity sat back up he reached with his right hand to gently fondle her left breast.

"Hey, you," she said and laughed quietly.

"I can talk now," Shadow said. "I'm awake."

"I can tell!" Laughing again she pushed his hand away.

"Take your blouse off so I can really look at you."

"Okay."

She slid her arms from the sleeves and dropped the blouse onto the bed beside Shadow.

"You're a fantastic looking woman," he said.

"I know. You're a fairly decent looking guy."

"Yeah, thanks. But my head aches like a son of a bitch. Who the hell did this to me? What the hell happened at the tavern?"

"I talked to the guys after they brought you back. They think some gang from somewhere, nobody knows where, wants to find grows around here and rip the mature plants off. Sunbeam says they might be from up north. Somebody else, Toon I think, or Shakespeare, says maybe they came from down south. I guess that leaves east and west. I can't remember who said what. Some shots were fired. Did you know that? I heard it. Nobody got hit or anything. But I've been all fucked up worrying about you. I still am."

"That's all you know? All you heard?"

"Somebody said they think some old dude who lives out by Cedar Creek in the cabin has something to do with it. Case? Is that his name? Hell, there's rumors everywhere. Somebody said maybe he got that gang up here. Shakespeare told me he heard it someplace. I think it was Shakespeare. Maybe it was somebody else. All Shakespeare ever really worries about is that Superpenis book he's writing."

"Ol' Superpenis. Oh yeah."

"How are you really? How bad's your head?"

"You know how your head feels the morning after you drink about three bottles of cheap red wine? Maybe four bottles?"

"No I don't."

"Well that's how my head feels anyway. It'll go away. We got any Advil?"

"Yeah we do. Sure."

"Would you please get me some?"

Shadow felt the bed move when Charity got up. "Be right back," she said and turned and walked away.

Now she wore only her white bikini panties. Shadow was afraid to move his head but he followed her out of the room with his eyes. When she disappeared through the door he closed his eyes and waited for the Advil.

When he heard Charity walking back into the room he opened his eyes. She was halfway from the doorway to the bed with a glass of water in one hand and a small white plastic bottle in the other. The bed moved again when she sat down.

"How many you want?"

"Four I guess. Fuck it. Make it five."

GROWER'S MARKET

Charity put the glass of water in his right hand. He stared at her breasts and heard her rattle the Advil out of the bottle.

"Here," she said.

Shadow took the tablets in his left hand and dropped them into his mouth and tried not to move his head when he swallowed water. Some of the cold water spilled down his chin and onto his chest but he got the Advil down. When the water spilled he remembered trying to feed amber ale to Uncle Sam.

SHAKESPEARE

He tried hard not to think about some things he had done as a boy. School was the only world he liked even though he had never been anything but bored in any of the schools he attended. When he was seventeen years old his English teacher Mr. Koch who was of course called Kochsucker by most of the boys in the class explained that William Shakespeare's plays had appealed to the masses and were bawdy. The boy who would later call himself Shakespeare wrote it off as another lame teacher's trick and went on daydreaming. But he did remember. A few years later he was riding home from a bar late at night in a friend's car and after accidentally running over the mayor's poodle the friend was pulled over for doing ninety in a thirty-five and driving under the influence and reckless driving. Because of the mayor's dead dog the friend was sentenced to thirty days in the county jail and even though Shakespeare had been asleep when the arrest was made he served five days for "aiding and abetting." In his cell he discovered a dog-eared paperback edition of three of William Shakespeare's plays under the filthy mattress on his bunk.

There was little else to do so he read through the plays twice and realized Kochsucker had told the truth. William Shakespeare had been bawdy. He had written about sex and had told dirty jokes and hundreds of years after his death millions of people all across the world read and attended his plays and studied them in classes. It could happen again. It was time now for a sophisticated and bawdy novel with relevant modern themes. It was time for a twenty-first-century Shakespeare.

Not long after beginning work on *Superpenis* Shakespeare had moved into a residence forty miles directly west of the Bird of Prey. The ramshackle four-room cabin he rented sat deep in a pine forest next to a half-acre pond stocked with bluegills and largemouth bass. The bluegills spawned prolifically and there were also frogs in the pond so the bass fed voraciously and grew large quickly.

Nearly every day Shakespeare spent an hour or more fishing the pond with top-water plugs and he ate fresh bass fillets for dinner most nights of the week from spring through fall. For an occasional change he fished with Elk Hair Caddis dry flies and ate bluegill fillets instead.

Shakespeare's principal reason for choosing the cabin had been that it brought him close enough to civilization to provide a reliable landline telephone. When he wasn't cultivating or harvesting a grow or fishing or working on *Superpenis*—writing his first draft with a quill pen he had discovered in an antique shop—he spent hours typing letters and chapters to send to the offices of literary agents and publishers in New York and elsewhere.

He included his phone number with his return address. He planned on finishing *Superpenis* in six months or at the very most a year or a year and a half and he felt he had to find a publisher. He knew a computer would have made things far easier for him but he called himself Shakespeare and refused to use one. Working on an old portable Royal typewriter he mailed the letters along with two sample chapters out as quickly as he could produce them. He would have written the letters and copied the chapters with the quill pen but realized it was unlikely anyone would read such copies. The drive to the nearest rural post office was ninety miles on slow roads and Shakespeare had made the trip more times than he could count.

On the morning after the Bird of Prey brawl he was casting a black and green plug called a Tap Dancer onto the pond and retrieving at various speeds but so far no bass had moved to it. The knuckles of both his hands were sore and bruised from busting heads at the tavern but he had no trouble casting the plug. Maybe the reason the bass weren't moving was that the fall nights had lowered the water temperature too low for warm water fish but now at 10:35 a.m. the sun had risen well above the treetops and its light and warmth reached the pond. That might help but even if it didn't the heat felt good on Shakespeare's back and shoulders. Ten yards behind him the cabin door was propped open with a stove chunk of firewood so he could hear when the phone rang. The editor from Bachus Books in New York was supposed to have called at 10 a.m.

Shakespeare made an arcing cast far across the calm water and watched the plug drop and land inches from a thick tree stump that protruded from the calm surface. Sometimes turtles climbed to the top of the stump to sun themselves. He let the plug sit until the last ring of water made by its landing had dissipated and then on the second crank of the reel as he began his retrieve a huge silver-sided bass shot up from somewhere underneath the log and flashed past the plug and came all the way out of the water in a long arc and then fell back with a loud splat and disappeared.

"Son of a bitch!" Shakespeare said.

Shading his eyes with his left hand he scanned the water where the bass had vanished but saw nothing through the sun's reflected glare. He reeled in at full speed with the Tap Dancer plug skimming the surface. That had been a ten-pound bass or maybe even twelve. That had been the biggest bass he'd ever seen here in the pond or anywhere.

With shaking hands Shakespeare aimed carefully and made another cast. He wanted to land the plug next to the log again but this time it hit the log and one of the treble hooks snagged in the porous wood.

He reeled in quickly and tightened his line and yanked hard but the plug wouldn't pull free. *"Shit!"* he said. *"Fuck!"*

Then the phone rang in the cabin.

"Son of a bitch!" he said.

He threw the rod down and sprinted into the cabin and reached the phone on the fourth ring and said, "Hello?"

"Mr. Shakespeare?"

"That's me!" Shakespeare said. "Speaking!"

"Well, well," said the same deep voice he remembered well from yesterday's voice message. "I never thought I'd actually have the opportunity to converse with William Shakespeare. In fact, I thought you were dead."

"Not me," Shakespeare said. "I'm not William Shakespeare. *You* know that. *I'm* not dead."

"What *is* your first name, Mr. Shakespeare?"

"I don't use my old names, my regular names. Not anymore I don't. Just plain Shakespeare."

"I see. Well, yes, I do. I think I do. Now. We've read your letter along with your sample chapters with considerable interest."

Shakespeare didn't know what to say so he didn't answer.

A lengthy pause followed.

"Hello?" said the deep voice. "Are you still there?"

"Oh yeah, I am!"

"My name is Meat. It derives from my career as a performer in the adult film industry, from which I'm recently retired."

"Meat?"

"Yes, as in a prime steak. Meat. So, shall we settle down to business?"

"Yeah!" Shakespeare's heart pounded. "Yes!" He had forgotten all about the monster bass.

"We find your character intriguing. I find him intriguing. Fascinating. Stimulating. I'm a senior editor here by the way. Don't get sanguine, though, please don't, but I think it's possible, not necessarily probable, but *possible* that we might do some business with you. Superpenis does intrigue us here at Bachus Books. The character does. We just might be able to sell him. *If* you give us what we need. This book would come out under our Firm Core imprint I should add. Have you possibly seen any of our Firm Core products, such as our current Studley Hungwell graphic novels? We have three different writers at work on that popular series with our art department going overtime! Mr. Hungwell's become quite the hero! Not just in America either! Have you seen him? Heard about him? There's no reason your hero couldn't be next!"

Shakespeare briefly considered lying but he'd never heard of either Firm Core or Studley Hungwell and had no idea what an art department had to do with novels. He couldn't conjure up a safe lie so another lengthy pause followed.

"Are you still there?" asked Meat.

"Yeah, I am! Yes!"

"Would you like me to tell you what we need?"

"Yeah! Yes! Please!"

"First, a new name for your character. Superpenis needs to become Supercock. You need to work in the commonly used vernacular. Do you follow me?"

"But it's crude, sir. 'Cock' is I mean."

"It's the standard twenty-first-century vernacular. And we need other substantial changes as well."

"Like what?"

"We need lots of fucking."

"Fucking?"

"Fucking," repeated Meat. "We needn't be delicate about this. What are male organs for? Fucking, right? Obviously they're necessary for urination, and just as obviously a cock can be pleasured in various and sundry ways, but the heart of it all is fucking. Fucking sells books under our Firm Core imprint. If it's *done* right, that is. In the material you sent there's no indication that Superpenis—or let's now call him Supercock—uses his organ as it's meant to be used. Tell me what you think. Explain, please."

"Explain?"

"Explain."

"I can't *explain* exactly."

"Why not? Is your character going to use his cock to fuck with, or isn't he?"

"He...I mean...I want..."

"*What* do you mean? *What* do you want? Tell me. Please explain."

"What I mean is, sir, Mr. Meat, is on one level I want *The Adventures of Superpenis* to be a *parody.* It's like I'm making fun of superheroes, get it? But there's another level, see? Readers who maybe aren't so sophisticated can take him seriously too, as a superhero, you know? I mean, I started out taking him totally seriously but then I kind of realized right away it had to be a parody too. It's got a whole other level of sophistication. Of complexity. Okay? It's like I'm making fun of all the guys who always worry about the size of their cocks. Their penises. See what I mean? I mean, like, it even has to do with wars. Like when America gets into all its useless wars it's like the country's measuring its cock. Its penis. See what I mean?"

"You're going to have to explain what the size of a penis—a cock—anybody's penis or cock—has to do with America's wars."

"Sure, I can explain! You know about LBJ, right?"

"I assume you're referring to Lyndon Baines Johnson, our thirty-sixth president."

"Right, Mr. Meat! Exactly! LBJ and the Vietnam War!"

"Well, what about LBJ and the Vietnam War, Mr. Shakespeare?"

This was a subject Shakespeare felt secure and confident about. "I bet you didn't know this, Mr. Meat," he said. "Ol' LBJ named his penis, his cock, 'Jumbo'! I do my research, I read all about it! He even showed his cock off sometimes, bragged about it, to reporters out on his ranch down there in Texas! See what I'm getting at? Ol' LBJ did some good shit, like civil rights, Medicare, but Jumbo, his penis—his cock—fucked him up in the end. Fucked *all* of us up. I mean he had this hang-up about how big Jumbo was, so you got to figure that was pure one hundred percent Texas macho bullshit that made him keep going with that useless fucking war. He wouldn't get out of that war, *couldn't* get out of that war, 'cause of Jumbo! Listen to this! One time when a reporter asked LBJ why we were still in Vietnam, he unzipped his fly and whipped out Jumbo and waved it around and told the guy, 'See this? *This* is why!' See what I'm saying, Mr. Meat? Lots of times it's macho-big cock bullshit that makes wars happen! That proves it! It's sure as shit what made Vietnam happen! Made it keep going! Iraq too! What I figure about Iraq is, maybe Bush Junior's cock was too little instead of big, but it all relates! See what I'm saying? It's complex! See what I mean? So what I'm mostly saying is, a sophisticated parody can get across important stuff about all *kinds* of subjects, even wars! Different levels of complexity can cover *everything*. I want my novel to cover it *all!*"

"A parody. Sophistication. Levels of complexity. I think I might understand where you're coming from. Tell me, Shakespeare, don't you suppose superheroes in a complex story, in a parody, or for that matter a nonparody, can fuck? Multifaceted people in complicated situations do it too, don't they? And—I've done a fair amount of research myself—I'm certain we can safely assume that LBJ did plenty of fucking."

"I guess so," Shakespeare said after another pause. "Yeah. Sure they do. Sure he did. Yes, sir. Sure they could. I guess."

"Well then why shouldn't Supercock fuck?"

"Yeah. Yes. I see what you mean, sir."

"Let me make myself clear. The original Shakespeare wrote racy scenes centuries ago. His characters fucked, though I grant not onstage. But they did indeed fuck. We live in a freer era now. Here in America we have the First Amendment. And consider some modern examples. I'm speaking of real people, in life, not literature. Consider any number of American presidents as public examples. Obviously we have European political leaders as well. If fucking was good enough for all of them, why can't it be good enough for Supercock?"

"Yeah. Yes. I guess I see what you mean, sir."

"Well if you see what I mean I'll proceed. Our readers like to read about fucking. Your character, Supercock as we'll call him now, suggests myriad possibilities. We'd very much like you to take advantage of those possibilities."

"Myriad?"

"With an endlessly stretchable plastic cock, *any*thing would be possible. Things that aren't even remotely possible on videos or in film. That's the real point here. We're a competitive market. Your character could give us an edge over our various competitors.

That's what makes the hero appealing, what gives your work its possibilities. Do you understand?"

"Yeah. Yes. Yes, sir."

"Here then is exactly what we'd like you to accomplish for us. For the time being. Please think this over carefully. Take your time. Take, let's say, three or four weeks. In about a month we'd like you to send us four scenes featuring your character, Supercock, in sexual scenarios. In plain language, we want him to do some serious and imaginative fucking. We want to see what you can come up with fucking-wise. Get me? I could make suggestions, but I'm assuming you understand me. Am I correct in that assumption?"

"Yes, sir, Mr. Meat. I guess I could have him fuck ten or twenty times if you want. Thirty or *forty*. Sure I could!"

"Eventually that will be just fine, if this works out. For now—in about a month that is—you send us four sex scenes, four fucking scenes, with Supercock in action. We'll evaluate your scenes and proceed from there. Understood?"

"Yes, sir!"

"He can continue to function as a hero, a superhero. If you choose to regard your story as parody, feel free. Those ideas needn't necessarily change, but the central focus must change. A stretchable plastic cock is an inspired idea! Genius! But we'll worry about all that later. Tell me, Shakespeare—tell me if you don't mind—what do you do for a living way out west?"

After a thoughtful pause Shakespeare answered, "A farmer. I'm a farmer out here."

"A farmer? In other words you grow things?"

"Yes, sir."

"Interesting. But what?"

"What?"

"What do you grow?"

After another pause Shakespeare answered, "Crops. Different crops. All kinds of stuff. Stuff people *want*."

After yet another pause Meat changed the subject. "Where exactly do you live?"

"I'm way out in the sticks, sir. *Way* out. Lots of mountains around! Rivers and lakes too!"

"I see. How old are you?"

"Thirty-three! Thirty-*four* I mean."

"Have you lived way out there in the sticks for very long? Tell me something about yourself. Were you born and raised there?"

Shakespeare welcomed the question. Most of his friends had heard him talk about the few parts of his life he cared to acknowledge but only Toon knew the truth and here now was an editor three thousand miles away who he could freely lie to. This was his chance to invent a life a manly writer could be proud of.

"I think I was born in San Francisco," Shakespeare began, speaking almost breathlessly now. "At least I heard I was. I guess my parents were hippies, you remember them, sure, everybody does, or at least heard about 'em, but I never met my parents, I never even knew who the hell they were, 'cause I got raised in a commune. *Different* communes I mean. I got raised by, like, about a hundred different folks, mostly women, but some men too, at least, like, a *few* men. I *heard* about different people who *might've* been my parents but nobody knew for sure, an' I heard my mom was like stoned all the time after some dude knocked her up but nobody knew for sure. I heard my old man was a poet who was stoned all the time too but I never saw his poems if he really ever wrote any. How could I see his poems? I never knew who the hell he was. I grew up all up and down the coast. I spent *lots* of time down in Mexico. *Some* time up north, but all I remember up there is it was cold an' rainy but Mexico was, like, *beautiful*! I mean, like, we lived on beaches down there in the sun! I went to some high schools though and read books, you know, growing up an' all. I was a tough kid in high school. I was tough anywhere I went. I was so big and strong everybody was scared of me. Still am big and strong. But what the hell, I even read Shakespeare! The only reason I joined the army was I couldn't find me a respectable damn job. I wanted to go to college and study creative writing an' the army promised me money to do it so I joined up and damn near got my ass blown off but afterwards, after I got set loose from the hospital, I went to a college an' they taught me how to write there an' now I got me my superhero Supercock! My parody!"

When Shakespeare paused for a breath Meat broke in. "Very interesting," he said. "Very intriguing. Your level of prose seems potentially adequate for our Firm Core imprint. But do remember! Supercock has to do some serious fucking! Is that clearly understood?"

"Yes, sir! *Serious* fucking, sir!"

"All right then, Shakespeare. We'll expect to hear from you in a month. Good-bye."

"Yes, sir, good-bye," Shakespeare said.

He felt his heart pounding as he lowered the phone from his ear and looked at it and then hung up.

Thinking over the conversation with Mr. Meat he walked across the cluttered room and back out the open door and before he reached his spinning rod lying among the tall weeds that grew at the edge of the pond he had his first misgivings.

Bachus Books with their Firm Core imprint wanted him to sell out. That was exactly what it amounted to. That was what the retired porn star Meat had told him he had to do. A senior editor named Meat wanted him to change Superpenis's name to Supercock and he wanted his character changed from a superhero in a parody to a sex fiend with a plastic cock.

Shakespeare bent over and picked up his rod. The Tap Dancer plug at the end of the monofilament line was still snagged on the tree trunk and he grasped the reel handle and backed up toward the cabin until the tightened line snapped. He threw the rod down and stood there staring out across the pond at the black and green Tap Dancer dangling from the tree stump a couple inches above the waterline.

The twenty-first century needed a parody about superheroes and big penises and war and politics but Meat told him he had to write four serious fuck scenes in a month. He didn't know if he should do it or even if he could do it if he wanted to. The world needed a superhero parody about wars and businessmen and politicians and now Meat and his Bachus Books with their Firm Core imprint wanted him to sell out.

Fuck no he wouldn't do it.

Shakespeare picked up the spinning rod and threw it down again harder than he had the first time and he turned and walked back to the three rickety wooden steps that led up to the cabin door. He sat on the top step with his boots in the weeds and his elbows on his knees and looked back across the pond at the snagged Tap Dancer and wondered what he should do.

If he turned his superhero into nothing but a dude with a stretchable plastic cock who fucked he was damn sure nothing but a sellout. But if he didn't change Superpenis into what they wanted the book might never get published. If he compromised he'd be a sellout and if he didn't compromise nobody would ever know about Superpenis, and that would definitely suck. He'd already mailed dozens of letters with chapters out and this was the first time anyone had responded and now he had to figure out what he should do.

SHAKESPEARE'S COVER LETTER

Dear Mr., Mrs., Ms., Editor, whatever:

I'm currently working very hard on a serious novel that I believe deserves your consideration. The first two chapters are included with this letter. My story is not only fast-paced and exciting but extremely meaningful as well. As you will see when you read this submission, my extraordinary hero confronts and bravely and resourcefully overcomes the sorts of people who are making life difficult, sometimes impossible, in the U.S.A. today.

I've been a student, a soldier, and a worker. My travels and experiences have allowed me to observe the villains my novel's hero contends with, the kinds of people who need to be understood and overcome if citizens hope to live free and satisfying lives. The plain truth is there are too many corrupt political leaders around, and greedy businessmen, and power-hungry military officers—in short, too many swindlers, thieves, con men, hypocrites, rich scumbags, and low-life motherfuckers.

I definitely believe that the way my hero thwarts these despicable people can be appreciated by readers of all kinds.

Sincerely,
Shakespeare

NVMBER 4 THOR

TOON

For as far back as he could remember Toon had been infatu-ated with comic books and the Sunday funnies and movie and television cartoons. Then as a twelve-year-old he began researching characters that were popular before his time. He read everything he could find about Popeye and Dick Tracy and Little Orphan Annie and Joe Palooka and Li'l Abner and The Katzenjammer Kids and Jiggs and Maggie and Gasoline Alley and Mutt and Jeff and Superman and Spiderman and Plastic Man and Captain Marvel and more. He firmly believed that sooner or later cartoons would be accepted as the one truly great American art form. Jazz might be accepted too but cartoons would be for sure. On a field trip with a high school class he visited American Indian dwellings and the etchings and paintings he saw on the walls of lava rock caves changed his life. He found himself imagining the way the Indians had lived with their hunting and fishing and dancing and chanting and drumming and warring. Sometimes he dreamed he was an Indian living a life of freedom that now was gone forever from earth. He especially envied the men who had made the cave *paintings. While most of the braves brought down deer with their bows and arrows and speared fish and fought battles there remained the lucky creative few who stayed home and painted scenes celebrating these activities. Toon wanted to paint in caves but no one lived in caves so of course no one painted in them anymore. One night as he sat alone in a bar drunk on tequila the answer hit him. He downed one last shot of Jose Cuervo and then walked six blocks down the street and got his first tattoo depicting Elmer Fudd chasing Bugs Bunny across his chest. He had been born too late to paint in caves so he would become the cave himself.*

Finally Toon decided to go ahead and have Dagwood Bumstead and Mr. Dithers tattooed on the cheeks of his ass. Once the tatts had been applied an observer behind him at a place like the Cedar Creek hot springs where everybody swam nude would see Mr. Dithers wearing a bright blue business suit and an orange shirt and a yellow necktie on the left cheek and Dithers would be running hard holding an upraised meat cleaver with a furious snarling look on his old man's face. On the right cheek would be Dagwood Bumstead wearing a tracksuit and fleeing in wide-eyed panic with his skinny arms outstretched. The tracksuit would consist of a black-and-white striped singlet and shorts meant to suggest a prisoner's outfit.

Under the warm morning sunlight Toon sat on a Coleman camp chair beside a fire pit encircled by large rocks and containing a charred black log resting on a gray bed of ashes damp from recent rain.

There were two daddy longlegs standing motionless next to each other on the damp ashes next to the log. Toon looked from the pair of spiders back at the sketchpad on his lap. For nearly an hour he had been laboring hard over a pencil drawing of Dagwood. When he had the drawing right he would fill in the colors with felt pens and start on Mr. Dithers. But he was far from satisfied with Dagwood whose head seemed too big and fat for his scrawny body. Toon couldn't even get the hair right. The two tufts that stuck out looked more like horns than hair. And Dagwood's legs that were meant to be running looked like limp spaghetti noodles sticking into over-sized shoes. Despite their Nike "swoosh" emblems the shoes looked like dead fish.

Toon couldn't remember if swooshes appeared on both sides of Nike shoes or only on the outsides. He wasn't sure because he didn't wear Nikes himself and had nothing at hand to go by. He tried to envision runners he had seen and finally guessed that the swooshes appeared on the outsides only so he erased the swoosh from the inside of Dagwood's left shoe and decided it looked better that way. The swooshes were crucial because they identified the Nike company that paid its overseas workers shit wages and treated them like slaves in order to produce their overpriced junk.

Toon glanced at his watch and saw he had barely an hour left to work on his sketches before he would have to leave if he hoped to reach Marlene's Tattoo Valhalla on time. He knew Mr. Dithers would be tougher to draw than Dagwood and he couldn't allow Marlene to work on him until he was able to give her sketches of exactly what he wanted and he had to sketch from memory because last week's Sunday funnies had been burned three or four days ago in his woodstove.

For now Toon concentrated on Dagwood's spaghetti-noodle legs. He erased what he had and tried again and erased again and tried yet again. No matter how tough this was he knew it would be more than worth the work. Dagwood getting bossed around and treated like shit by Mr. Dithers was the same way enlisted men got bossed around and treated like shit by their NCOs and officers. Toon's tattoo would express what he wanted to tell the future about the way life used to be on planet earth.

Toon knew a good deal about the history of tattoos. Decorative body images had existed for thousands of years and were observed for the first time by white men during south sea voyages. Captain Cook had seen tattoos in Hawaii or Samoa or maybe it had been Hawaii *and* Samoa. He didn't know for sure about Captain Cook but long before Cook's time tattooing had been practiced by Germanic and Celtic tribes in northern Europe. In modern times it was sailors who had made tattooing popular. Soldiers on both sides in America's Civil War sported tatts and soldiers still liked them and Toon had known men who used tatts to record permanent records of battles and kills. He had known a corporal who had a checkmark tattooed on his right arm for every enemy soldier he killed and an X on his left arm for every civilian he needlessly murdered, and he had accumulated almost twice as many Xs as checkmarks when a sniper killed him with a bullet through the throat.

After taking some of the bend out of Dagwood's legs Toon was finally satisfied with them but now the Nike shoes at the ends of the legs looked more like dead fish than ever. The swoosh mark on the right shoe looked like a horizontal gill slit. He erased both dead fish and started over on them.

Toon thought with satisfaction about Marlene's colored ink injected through his epidermis into his dermis. Since his army days he had regarded the world as nothing more or less than a gigantic slaughterhouse. Earth was a globe spinning through space and crowded with creatures constantly tormenting one another. If it wasn't an animal like a coyote hounding a bird like a roadrunner or a first sergeant screaming at a private first class it was an asshole businessman like Mr. Dithers making life miserable for a hopeless innocent nerd like Dagwood Bumstead.

Toon's butt cheeks would show what he thought about what he'd experienced and seen. Researchers and archeologists discovered dead bodies thousands of years old and sometimes the dug-up bodies had tattoos. If there was anyone around to dig Toon up in a thousand years or ten thousand years or *twenty* thousand years he wanted his tatts to prove he'd seen what was happening on earth and had recorded it during his lifetime on his own skin.

There. He believed he finally had it. Dagwood's Nikes were okay including the swooshes. Next came the hair and when he got that right he could start on Mr. Dithers.

If everything worked out he'd get the tattoos this afternoon and keep bandages on them for two or three hours and then peel off the tape and gauze and let the fresh air do its work. He'd have to keep his ass dry for at least two weeks and keep it out of the sun for three weeks. Keeping his ass out of the sun would be easy enough. For a few days sitting down might be a problem but he could use soft pillows even on the toilet seat. He'd sleep on his stomach and during the days he'd be working on his feet so he could still do his job at the grows.

No sooner had Toon begun work on Dagwood's hair than all his plans for the day were ruined. He heard the ATV coming from half a mile or more away and his shoulders slumped and his eyes narrowed and he stopped his work and listened as the harsh mechanical sound grew gradually louder. He knew it had to be somebody from last night coming to give him some bad news.

Shrimp came riding out of the trees and roared straight across the clearing and skidded to a stop a few feet from the fire pit. He wore a zipped up black leather jacket and a black New York Yankees baseball cap.

Suddenly the cool air stank of exhaust fumes.

"Hey, Dude," Shrimp said with a casual wave.

"What's up?" asked Toon.

"We got to meet at the tavern," Shrimp said. "Right away."

"What the fuck for?"

"There's more weird shit happening. Sunbeam wants to see us, now."

"What weird shit?"

"I guess that's why she wants to see us, to tell us about it."

"Shit," said Toon. "I had plans, man. Im*port*ant plans!"

"Me too. *Damn* important. But we got to go."

"I guess we're fucked."

"Yeah we are."

* * *

Fly tying enabled Case to forget his aches and pains and he often thought that more than anything else he did it kept him relatively sane. He sat at his tying table set against the biggest window in his living room. From his chair he could look through the clean glass across the sugar pine table westward at the half-acre plot where the vegetable garden used to be and behind the garden the orchard of apple and pear and cherry trees and then the wall of big trees that were mostly Douglas firs that stretched across a mile of nearly level ground to steep mountains that except for their clear-cuts were beautiful to see.

If he had been looking through the window today Case might have noticed the two figures dressed in camouflage fatigues making their slow and careful way out of the fir trees into the orchard. Crouching with shotguns carried at port arms they moved quickly from tree to tree through the orchard. They used the largest trees to conceal themselves and whenever they stopped behind the big trees they looked at the cabin before darting forward again. Every time they hid themselves they looked at one another and occasionally one would lift his hand from his weapon to give a signal. They knew Case was inside and had agreed beforehand that if he happened to see them and then confront them they would claim to be quail hunters chasing a running covey.

But Case didn't see them because he had quit the view to tie up steelhead flies for the fall run. The fish had to travel hundreds of miles upstream from the sea to reach this country and the first ones should arrive in a week or two or three weeks at the latest. Case often thought of himself as he thought of the coastal rivers. They were dying but they weren't dead yet. A good fall rain would raise the water and bring whatever fish were destined to come more quickly. Whenever they arrived Case would be ready. His reels were greased and his leaders were built and now he was tying Thors.

He used needle-nose pliers to crimp the barb down on a number 4 hook and then clamped the hook into the vise. With the thread bobbin gripped in his right hand he wrapped the shank from the upturned eye to the bend of the hook and then tied in a half-inch length of bright orange wool for the tail. Most tyers preferred a tuft of orange hackle fibers for Thor tails but Case knew wool showed up better underwater. Next he tied in a length of heavy red chenille and then he wrapped the shank of the hook with the chenille and tied it off. Next came the brown hackle and finally the flared white bucktail wing. He carefully trimmed the excess bucktail with a small sharp pair of scissors. He formed the slender head with tying thread and finally applied the clear head cement with a needle. Then he unclamped the finished fly and stuck it into the edge of the table to dry. The wood along the table edge was marked with thousands of tiny indentations left by Thors and Muddlers and Skunks and Golden Demons and Alaska Mary Anns.

Case didn't hear the discharge of the shotgun. The window burst in his face and hot air along with shards and fragments of glass flew past him. Some of the glass hit him. Luckily he had been bent over a new hook in the vise so nothing caught his face. All he heard was the blast of air and the glass sailing past his ears and he felt the bits of glass that imbedded in his arms and chest and the top of his head and he felt shock rather than pain.

He lay on his back on the floor behind the fly-tying table and blinked his eyes and saw the ceiling overhead. He blinked and stared at the varnished knotty pine planks so he knew he could see and he felt the chair he had been sitting in with his feet and he looked at his bare forearms and saw a lot of blood but not enough to worry about.

He felt the warm blood running down his face and neck and he rolled onto his stomach and pushed to his feet. He stood bent at the waist until the room stopped wobbling and spinning. Then he straightened up and wiped his face and looked at his blood-smeared hands and then he looked at his fly-tying table. He looked for the Thor he had finished and saw the undamaged fly where he had stuck it to the table's edge.

SIP AND HITS

CANNABIS

The established cannabis growers in these parts were old-time self-taught experts in a competitive and constantly evolving enterprise. There were principles that growers held to firmly and they felt the same kind of pride in successful crops that winemakers feel about good years in their vineyards. Crops should never be raised indoors with diesel-powered generators supplying artificial light but should grow under the sun as nature intended without the use of pesticides or anything but the purest organic fertilizers. These growers planted and cultivated and harvested and patrolled against invading rippers on foot, with little or no dependence on the four-wheelers and Rhinos utilized in many other places. Some of them had been on the cannabis scene since before the emergence of sinsemilla in the 1970s. They knew all the strains and all the possible crosses between Cannabis sativa and Cannabis indica and had devised the best possible methods for picking and trimming and drying. Over the years through painstaking experimentation they created their own unique strains that were now as potent as the famed Jack Flash and Bubble Gum and just as desirable on the open market. Thousands of

*wounded and maimed vets who came home depended on cannabis to
reduce their physical and mental misery. Some used it to manage the
terrible pains they experienced in phantom as well as existent limbs
and many, including the wounded, joined in production and sales.*

With two hours to go until the official opening time, the Bird
of Prey smelled faintly and not unpleasantly of beer and tobacco
and cannabis smoke and cleanser and floor polish. All the
wooden shutters were closed tight so the only illumination came
from neon signs mounted high on the wall behind the long bar.
The signs advertised light beer that hardly anyone bought and
a popular mass-produced beer that even fewer people bought
because most of the tavern's regular patrons knew that the man
who founded the brewery had been an ignorant right-wing asshole. Bird of Prey regulars were loyal to the microbreweries that
produced amber ales and pale ales and oatmeal stouts rich with
flavor. The principal reason Sunbeam stocked a few cases of
mass-produced beers was so she could keep a close eye on any
customer who bought them.

This morning all the blood had been scrubbed away and the
pinewood floor had been mopped and waxed and buffed. The bar
had been wiped down and sanitized and the shelves and walk-in
cooler were stocked and the grill where the late-night buffalo
burgers were cooked had been scrubbed hard with a soapy wire
brush.

Sitting at the same table in the same chair she had used last
night Sunbeam had finished her usual breakfast of scrambled

eggs and buttered whole-wheat toast and hash browns doused with Tabasco. Rainbow had cleared Sunbeam's dirty dishes away and was working behind the bar across the room while Sunbeam thought about the outsiders who had Pearl-Harbored her establishment. The outsider scumbags had molested and abused her customers and employees.

The big table was bare except for the white mug of steaming black coffee and her antique golden Dunhill lighter and the freshly lit four-inch joint balanced on the green glass ashtray directly in front of her. The smooth black tabletop showed faint smears left by a wet sponge, and a length of mop string had stuck between the bottom of one of Sunbeam's chair legs and the wooden floor. With her right hand she took an occasional sip of the coffee and always followed the coffee with a healthy left-handed hit from the joint. As she saw it the caffeine kept her sharp and the cannabis kept her mellow.

Pot helped keep Sunbeam calm and allowed her to think things through logically. What she had to figure out this morning was exactly the right way to keep her business empire safe and thriving, and that meant she had to harshly repel whoever was moving in on her and she had to do it now.

Bad things were happening almost everywhere in remote pot country and had been happening for years now and more frequently all the time. Growers who had lived in the woods for decades and had never wanted anything more than a fair amount of money and a quiet and simple life in a tranquil setting were getting pressured by greed-freaks who only cared about making all the money they could. The greed-freaks didn't want to live in cabins or simple homes or drive Toyotas or Subarus or spend a winter month or two in southern Baja. They wanted to drive BMWs or Lincoln Navigators and live in mansions with swimming pools and spend their vacations dining in Paris or sightseeing in Rome or touring Egypt or playing golf with other greed-freaks at Pebble Beach or on Maui.

Sunbeam couldn't remember exactly how many years ago they had started showing up in the backcountry with earthmovers and chainsaws and pesticides and fertilizers. Twelve years? Fifteen? From the very beginning they poisoned and desecrated the earth. They sucked water from clean cold trout streams for their irrigation and they guarded their grows with pit bulls and assault weapons. From everything she'd heard things were getting worse nearly everywhere. The worst kinds of violence had become commonplace. Two weeks back, or it might have been three, a bearded biker traveling south on a Harley had stopped at the tavern and casually mentioned to Sunbeam that he had heard up north that one of the big new greed-freak growers had firm plans to import men from Mexican drug cartels to help guard his grows.

"You're *really* out in the sticks, foxy ol' momma!" the biker had said. "This here's sure as shit *God's* country here! But sooner or later them bad-ass businessmen'll get to you too! The bad-asses're coming! You can mark my words on *that*!"

Now Sunbeam sipped her coffee and took another hit and held it in. The badasses were here but she wasn't sure just how bad they were. If she tried to drive them off she had to keep it quiet. Even as she contemplated protecting her space she knew she might not be capable of doing enough to stop what appeared to be coming. For two or three months now fat-assed Deputy Winter had seemed more nervous and more evasive than ever. Exactly how bad were the badasses? That was the question and thinking hard about it her puckered mouth resembled a cloth pouch with its string drawn tight.

Another sip of coffee along with another hit and her mind floated along. There were fleeting memories of both people and events from the past. Her life had really begun in San Francisco. She briefly considered the husband she had lived with for so many years. She rarely thought of him and she didn't miss him because he was gone and wasn't coming back and missing him made no sense. Sometimes she wondered whether her marriage had failed her or she had failed it. She couldn't decide and now it didn't matter anyway.

Now she wanted Case. His wife was dead and her husband was dead and she and Case were alive and she wanted them to get together and live together. Case was a good-looking older man and a smart and mature man and a fit man, and Sunbeam was certain that with her help he would still be able to perform. But perform wasn't the word because sex wasn't a play on a stage. Get it up. Yes. Get it up and use it well. Fuck. She too was considered old but Sunbeam knew she was fit and she had been attractive since puberty and she still wanted to fuck. Yes she still needed it and yes she hoped she always would.

Another sip and another hit.

If she could get Case she might just retire and let the greed-freaks have their way and choke on their money. She and Case could go somewhere. But she didn't think she could get Case. She knew she couldn't. She'd made it clear in the various ways women let men know such things that she was anxious to have him. She was anxious to get it on. But the harder she tried the less often he came around.

The last time Case had been in for an after-fishing beer had been within two or three days of the Harley rider who issued the warning. Sunbeam had walked up to the bar with her coffee mug in one hand and welcomed Case with her other hand pressed against his thigh and a quick kiss on his cleanly shaved cheek.

"Long time no see, dude," she said. "I've missed you."

She knew Case had spent hours wading the river and casting his flies and he still smelled like aftershave. He looked toward her but not quite at her and smiled and looked away. "Hello," was all he said.

The only other customers that afternoon had been a log-truck driver drinking coffee at the far end of the bar and four old hippies drinking beer and smoking pot at a table behind them. The log truck was parked out front pointed south under the sign and "The Devil to Pay" by Johnny Cash was playing on the jukebox.

"How come you're unfriendly?" Sunbeam asked Case.

"I'm not unfriendly," he said without looking at her after a sip of beer. "Good beer," he said. "Delicious."

"How come you don't like me?" Sunbeam asked him.

"I like you," Case said.

"I think you're lonely. I figure that's what's wrong. That's my humble opinion. You know you don't have to be lonely."

"My opinion is your opinion's wrong."

"Listen to me, Case. We're too old to bullshit each other. I want you to come down here to have dinner with me some night. You live, what, twenty miles away?"

"I think it's closer to eighteen."

"See there? Even less than I thought. Come by Thursday night, day after tomorrow. We're never very busy on Thursdays. We can have some dinner and talk. I have some good fresh salmon in the walk-in, just got it yesterday. You like salmon?"

"I like salmon fine."

"Moon Mac brought it in. It's Chinook. You know old Moon."

"Sure I do."

"Is it a date then?"

Case drank more beer. Sunbeam clearly saw that he felt uncomfortable. After swallowing the beer he wiped his mouth with the back of his hand and then began making designs of wet circles on the wooden bar with the bottom of his pint glass. "I'll come by if I can," he finally said. "But don't make any special preparations. I don't think I can make it, but I'll come if things work out."

Now the Johnny Cash song about Folsom Prison was playing.

"Make it seven o'clock," Sunbeam said. She put her hand back on Case's thigh and leaned close to kiss his cheek again. "I like you a hell of a lot," she said in his ear.

When Case made no response Sunbeam got up with her coffee and walked across the room and into her office and closed the door without looking back. She was angry and also smart enough to recognize her own shallow female vanity. She fully understood how stupid it was for old folks to descend into illogical forms of self-absorption yet despite all that she knew and understood she wanted Case. She needed him.

But he hadn't come for dinner Thursday night and she hadn't seen him since.

She knew Deputy Winter thought Case might be involved at some level in growing or selling weed but Sunbeam didn't believe it could be true and she wanted to talk to Case about Winter. Case might come into the place again sometime soon but she couldn't be certain of that. She might not see him for weeks. He liked to keep to himself and that was his problem.

Now Sunbeam carried her empty coffee mug across the room and slid it down the bar to where Rainbow was using a sharp narrow-bladed knife to slice green limes to serve with tequila. For some reason Sunbeam couldn't understand, tequila seemed to be getting more popular all the time. It was getting more expensive too and she could remember early times in Mexico when tequila cost little more than gasoline.

The clock over the jukebox read 10:55. Rainbow placed the knife on the bar and refilled Sunbeam's mug and carried it back. "Somebody's here for your meeting," she said. "They pulled into the lot just now."

"Who?" Sunbeam asked.

"I heard, I didn't see."

"Last night was pretty bad. Damn bad. Gunfire in the Bird of Prey. I don't like trouble but we might be having some serious shit around here. How's Uncle Sam doing?"

"This morning he's about as good as it gets. Shrimp talked to him last night. Shrimp's back again, up there right now, got here half an hour ago. He's a good man."

"Shrimp? Yeah he is." Sunbeam took a seat at the bar. "Tell me something, Rainbow."

"What?"

"That nurse who helped you out with Uncle Sam. Case's wife. Heather. Did you like her?"

"I liked her a lot. She was wonderful."

"I never got to know her. What was it made her wonderful?"

Rainbow continued slicing the limes as she spoke.

"Well for one thing she was wonderful with Uncle Sam. She got him to blink his eyes more than anybody else ever did. I don't know how she did it but she did. One thing was, she had a sense of humor. She could make a joke about anything. She always seemed happy. She liked what she did. I'd like to be a nurse myself someday. I plan on it. She's the one who gave me the idea."

"You nurse Uncle Sam every day."

"Oh, sure, I do. He's my husband. I love him. The truth is I don't know how long he'll live. Even if he lives a long time I'd like to nurse other people too. Heather said it was hard sometimes but it always made her happy. She was great. I like Case too. It hit him hard when she died."

"I know it did."

"Heather had a hard time. But she never complained and she never even lost her sense of humor. I still miss her. She really was great."

GROWER'S MARKET

Sunbeam stood up from the bar. "I guess she must have been. You're pretty great yourself, Rainbow. Don't you forget it."

Sunbeam carried the coffee back to her table and sat down. The roach had died in the ashtray so she fired up a fresh joint with the Dunhill and sat there waiting while alternating sips and hits.

A WILDERNESS TRAIL

Shakespeare had swerved off the road and slammed on his brakes and come to a skidding stop at the edge of the lot close beside one of the tall metal stanchions that held up the Bird of Prey sign. The only other vehicle there was Shrimp's Toyota and he figured Shrimp to be upstairs visiting Uncle Sam.

As always Shakespeare was a little early. Arriving ahead of time was an old army habit he'd never tried to break. He rolled both front windows down to catch the breeze and sat in the Bronco with both hands gripping the steering wheel as he pondered his Superpenis-cock dilemma. Since his phone conversation with Editor Meat of Bachus Books's Firm Core Imprint in New York he had thought of little else.

Shakespeare knew he had to invent the requested scenes and probably had to work quickly because otherwise they might well forget all about him in New York. Worse yet would be if they stole his idea and his character and gave it to another writer who would ruin what was rightfully his own. Editor Meat had told him there were three different writers working on Studley Hungwell books. That could mean that three writers or four or five could end up writing Supercock books.

The thought of New York and what went on there both frightened and disgusted Shakespeare. He'd never been anywhere near that huge city that represented nearly everything he thought he hated. When he thought of New York all he could imagine were millionaires and snobs and Wall Street swindlers and conceited bitches in fur coats and East Coast assholes in general. They were all people who'd never pissed in the woods or for that matter ever even been there.

And what if he did what he had to do and it all worked out and Bachus Books—Firm Core—published his novel and he had to actually travel to New York? Well then he'd go there and he'd deal with the New Yorkers when he had to. He'd known four or five New Yorkers during his army time and he kind of liked only one but the ones he didn't like hadn't bothered him much. He ignored the ones he didn't like and never got to know the one New Yorker who seemed all right because two weeks after that one shipped in and joined the company, a skinny little local urchin with explosives underneath his rags blew him and five other soldiers to bloody bits. Shakespeare hadn't even learned that one kind of decent New Yorker's name.

So he'd deal with New York and New Yorkers if he had to. There had to be good people there too. What mattered was that even if Supercock had to fuck he also had to be a hero and had to defeat Evil and on top of all that he had to be a parody of all the fake heroes invented by the Hollywooders and New Yorkers. The problem boiled down to why a hero should fuck in a parody and who he should fuck and where and when.

Shakespeare decided maybe Supercock should fuck just because he was a man and it was normal for him to want to do it at least once in a while. For that matter women also wanted to at least once in a while. But with Supercock it had to be because he was making fun of conquering evil. That was the hard part. He couldn't fuck only because he felt like it. It would be okay if he felt like it but there had to be more. Somehow fucking and defeating evil and making fun of defeating evil had to be neatly tied together.

In the last scene Shakespeare had written Supercock was at a rodeo and used his cock to lasso a steer. But now Shakespeare probably couldn't use the rodeo scene unless he could figure out a true motivation for Supercock to fuck while he was there. What if some crook or some scumbag was masquerading as a cowboy and had his Russian mistress with him? Make it one of those scumbags they called oligarchs. Shakespeare kept up with the news and knew that oligarchs were rich Russian assholes who put the screws to everybody else so they could make more money the same way rich assholes did it in America and pretty much everywhere else.

When a log truck heading north loaded with old-growth Douglas fir sped along the narrow road past the tavern the roaring blast of wind shook the Bronco. Shakespeare smelled the diesel exhaust and watched the truck and figured you could call the timber company bosses oligarchs. They paid off the politicians so they could rape the public land until it looked like some evil giant had pushed a colossal lawnmower up and down over the mountains. What those timber company oligarch bastards figured was fuck the trees and mountains and rivers and fuck the whole earth because all they wanted was money.

When the log truck disappeared Shakespeare remembered a rodeo he had attended years ago. The state's fat governor had showed up wearing a big white cowboy hat and shiny black cowboy boots and he made a long-winded speech at the opening ceremonies. It was a typical political speech crammed full of all the standard patriotic and religious bullshit. That was long before Shakespeare joined the army and what he remembered from the governor's speech now seemed much worse than it had when he first heard it.

But all these years later the fat governor gave him an idea. The Russian oligarch masquerading as a cowboy at the rodeo could own a timber company and be in cahoots with the governor about a modern-day logging rip-off. The governor could be like the asshole politician from back east who said he went hiking on a wilderness trail when he really was off in another country fucking his mistress. Okay. So the timber company oligarch asshole and the governor tell the press they're having a business meeting someplace secret but they're really on a wilderness trail fucking their mistresses. Supercock finds out about it and he's hiding somewhere out there on the wilderness trail waiting for the timber company oligarch asshole and the governor. When they show up Supercock can turn his cock into a rattlesnake and not any normal rattler either but one about fifteen feet long and as thick as a telephone pole. The giant rattler scares the shit out of the timber company oligarch and the governor and they take off running and never look back. When they're gone Supercock can give it to both mistresses better than they ever had it before because he can make his cock as big as he wants and he can do anything he feels like doing with it. He can use it like a drill or a jackhammer or a high-speed blender.

The jackhammer thought led to another idea. Shakespeare remembered a magazine article he'd read in a dentist's waiting room about a professional wrestler with an alter ego. An alter ago meant a person had a second self and whether he liked it or not led two lives instead of only one. The wrestler was called the Jerkhammer and the article compared him to Dr. Jekyll and Mr. Hyde. In real life the wrestler was known to be a kind and generous family man but as soon as he climbed into a ring he turned into the Jerkhammer and enjoyed attacking opponents from behind and gouging their eyes and strangling them and smashing their heads with metal folding chairs. So in his novel maybe Superpenis's alter ego could be Supercock. Supercock could do all the fucking and Superpenis could do the rest and with hard work and deep thinking Shakespeare could figure it out and satisfy Editor Meat and save his novel too.

"*Yes!*" Shakespeare said aloud and he pounded on the steering wheel with both hands.

Just then two more vehicles pulled into the lot simultaneously. One was an Isuzu Trooper from the south and the other a Subaru from the north.

"*Yes!*" Shakespeare said again. "*Sweet!*"

He rolled his windows up and climbed out of his Bronco to say hello to Shadow and Stones.

GROWER'S MARKET

* * *

Stones stepped out of his Subaru with his good eye strained and watering after a high-speed drive on hazardous roads back from the shelter. With a smile on his face he waved to his friends.

He had driven into town long before dawn and spent the early morning sanding wooden chairs and talking to Lan at the shelter. She sat behind her desk and he worked near the doorway that led to the shower room out back. He told her more about his life than he had ever told anybody. He included the football and the army and the wrestling and the nightclub and his brief time as a cop.

There were periodic interruptions. The phone rang three times and Lan told the callers where the shelter was and what it had to offer. An old man with a white beard came in for a shower and food. He carried his meager possessions in a black plastic garbage bag that was slung over his shoulder the way Santa Claus carries his sack of Christmas presents. While the old man was back in the shower a young couple with backpacks came in for food. They both wore jeans and sweatshirts. The boy was frail and looked troubled and the girl could have been a high school cheerleader. They loaded their packs with canned fruits and vegetables and didn't want showers.

When Stones had to go Lan walked him out to his car. She barely came up to his elbow.

Somewhere far away a dog was barking.

Stones sat in the driver's seat with the window open and the motor running and told Lan he wanted to try changing his life.

With both hands gripping the wheel he stared down the empty road. He told her he hated being big and strong because that was what had always steered him toward violence. He was sick of it and now he wanted something better.

"I'll try to help you," Lan said and she leaned into the car and kissed his cheek and quickly turned and walked away.

* * *

SHRIMP

He worried about the irrational fears that he commonly experienced. Before his war he had lived a carefree life. After high school graduation he made good money in the woods as a logger. In his free time he drank beer and chased women and hunted and fished. Then when logging in the over-cut forests slowed down to next to nothing he enlisted to earn college money. Now he was back from the war and everything was different. Without wasting time in college he earned better money than he'd ever dreamed of making, but he wasn't happy. When he drank beer he couldn't keep himself from wondering how beer glasses were made and whether there might be a chemical involved in their manufacture that would slowly poison him over the years. When he went steelhead or salmon fishing and hooked into a big one he feared that the fish would break off and escape because of a flaw in the monofilament line he was using. If he landed the fish he wondered if it might be contaminated with mercury. Wherever he was and whatever he was doing he often found it virtually impossible to acknowledge any form of happiness. If he started feeling good about something he soon concocted an idea to counteract his pleasure. A cold beer on a hot day or a delicious meal inevitably led to the idea that beer and food would make him fat and eventually cause diabetes or a heart attack. More than anything else in his life Shrimp wanted a woman to live with and to love but if he picked up a pretty girl at the Bird of Prey and took her home by the time they arrived at his place he had convinced himself she had to be diseased. He was certain that three tours of combat duty had a lot to do with his problems but he also thought there had to be something more and he couldn't figure out what it was. But he kept trying.

Shrimp sat staring down at what was left of Uncle Sam lying flat on his back with his clear brown eyes wide open.

"I wish you could understand what I say," Shrimp told him. "Maybe you can. At least *some* of it anyway. What I figure is maybe you can hear but you can't understand but maybe you like the sound of a human voice at least. That's okay, buddy. That's fine, dude. Blink if you can understand anything I say. Blink right now. Go on, man, do it!"

Uncle Sam didn't blink. He breathed slowly and deeply with his chest rising and falling beneath the red sheet with sunlight through the clean window hitting the left side of his pale face.

"Fuck it, dude," Shrimp said. "I'll keep talking anyway. Maybe you *do* like the sound of a voice. Ol' Shakespeare just pulled up and parked down in the lot. He's sittin' there in his rig waitin' on people. We got a meeting coming up in a while downstairs with Sunbeam. Somebody's invading our territory but nobody knows who it is. I don't even see why it matters who it is. I mean, everybody's territory gets invaded by somebody, right? Take a look at the world, right? Outsiders show up sooner or later every-place, right? You and me were a couple of the outsiders a while back. A couple fucking enlisted men. I sure do wish you could talk. You always were a smart dude compared to the rest of us. Maybe you could figure out what's up around here with all the turf war bullshit, all the greed-freaks. Oh yeah, in case you're hungry Rainbow'll be up here pretty quick with your breakfast. That's what she told me. Speaking of food, last night, midnight it was, some dude tried to stuff in ten buffalo burgers in half an hour. Never made it. Nobody ever does. Remember that army chow though? Didn't that shit suck? I remember those meals out at deer camp though. Sweet! Fresh cutthroat trout fried up in bacon grease. Or some elk tacos. Or maybe some venison jerky from last year's deer. A joint or two. Cold beer from the ice chest. Hey, Uncle Sam, Shadow and Stones just parked down in the lot too so I guess I got to head downstairs now for the big meeting. Blink for me, dude?"

Uncle Sam didn't blink.

Shrimp patted his shoulder. He stood and crossed the quiet room and went through the door and started down the stairs. Halfway down he ran into Rainbow coming up. She was using both hands to carry a tray with a bowl of oatmeal and a glass of orange juice and a mug of coffee on it. Shrimp turned and climbed back up to open the door for her.

"Thanks, Shrimp," she said.

"Looks like a decent breakfast," Shrimp answered.

"The only trouble is Uncle Sam usually soils himself bad after oatmeal."

When she walked through the door Shrimp closed it quietly behind her. He knew about Rainbow's life. How come good people like Rainbow got so much rotten luck? First she had to run off from home and then after a while she met Uncle Sam and married him and here she was now, and Shrimp often thought he could love her if she'd let him. But he knew that now, when he had a deep tan after a long summer, the plastic surgery scars showed on his face and he wondered if it mattered. He wondered if his scars grossed Rainbow out and if they did he knew she was too nice to talk about it. She was married to Uncle Sam and Shrimp thought he might love her and wondered what he should do. Whenever he tried to figure things out he felt like a man who'd got off a train at the wrong station with no idea where he started from or where he was or how he got there.

* * *

After blotting and wiping off the blood and taping the gauze bandages over his wounds Case worked methodically at cleaning up his place. He began by pushing and carrying furniture out of the room and then he walked down to the basement and found an old pair of work gloves and an empty cardboard box and carried the box back upstairs.

Wearing the gloves he carefully removed the jagged shards of glass that remained in the window frame. As he worked, warm blood trickled out from underneath a bandage and down his forehead into his left eye. He wiped it away with his sleeve. His head had stopped ringing and now it ached and throbbed. He noticed that the glass frames of several enlarged photographs had been destroyed along with the window. The photo he cared about most had been taken on a sunny Christmas Day and showed Heather on cross-country skis on a gentle hill down a mountain-side. The ski trail ran through old-growth firs and Heather was smiling and the bright blue sky showed behind her.

Case swept glass and debris into a pile in the corner nearest his fly-tying table and then used a dustpan to shovel everything into the cardboard box. The box was nearly full and heavy when he carried it downstairs to the garage.

Back upstairs again he used a wet dishtowel to wipe dust and flakes of paint and tiny glass fragments off the furniture. Every few minutes he had to soak the dishtowel and carefully ring it out and then wet it again and resume work. When everything was wiped down he put the furniture back where it belonged. There were scolding jays in the trees close to the cabin the whole time he worked and they sounded surprisingly loud with the window glass gone.

As he finished the work cruel memories flashed through his mind. There were hot wet jungles and hand grenades and mortar shells and a huge rat that had bitten his neck while he dozed, and the early morning after the rat fourteen of them had been outnumbered and attacked and they ran in panic through rifle fire and mortar explosions and eight of them made it to safety. The next afternoon they went back for their comrades. They went back through the heavy humid heat and the wet green vegetation under the dark sky and the first body they found was Case's closest army friend. He was a draftee nicknamed Horse and they found him propped up against a tree trunk sitting the way a man might rest in the shade on a hot day. He was naked with two bullets through the pale bloody chest and his hazel eyes were open and his throat had been slit and his nose and his ears had been cut off and his dick had been cut off and stuffed into his mouth. They soon found four more naked bodies and all had been mutilated in much the same ways. They looked hard for a long time but never found the sixth body.

Horse had been a handsome and quick-witted boy whose father taught high school Spanish and coached baseball. He was a college graduate and had planned to teach math and coach basketball after the army. Now he had been dead for more than forty years. For about half of those years Case had asked himself why men who didn't know each other killed each other and he'd never figured it out and finally gave up trying. They were men and they just did.

Case heard the silence when the jays in the trees stopped scolding.

Someone with a deep voice yelled from the forest: *"Stay home, old man! If you know what's good for you! If you're still in one fucking piece stay right where you fucking are!"*

Case walked out of the room and down the stairs to his living room where he kept a pair of Bushnell binoculars on the coffee table next to the big window there. He scanned the road that led up over the hill and saw no movement or sign of life and then he scanned the woods on both sides of the road and saw nothing but trees.

Back upstairs he looked again through the opening that had been the window. He saw nothing so sat back down at his table to tie another Thor. When he wrapped the number 4 hook with waxed black thread he was glad his hands weren't shaking. He knew he wasn't afraid.

As he worked on the Thor he remembered hiking with Heather across their favorite valley. They had picnicked at the edge of a vast meadow carpeted with wildflowers. He knew he could never again become the man he had been then. The chasm between the man he was then and what he was now was a valley that couldn't be crossed.

Case tied three more number 4 Thor steelhead flies. Each fly was meticulous and as close to perfect as he could make it. By the time the head cement was applied to the last Thor his headache was nearly gone and he knew that after lunch he'd be heading back to the country he'd been chased through yesterday to search for his abandoned backpack.

I SHOT THE SHERIFF

When Sunbeam found herself inescapably involved in a scheme that she knew was corrupt she often tried to take the edge off her culpability by using vulgar army sergeant language: "Drop your cocks and grab your socks," she told her group of veterans, "and let's get this maneuver on the road."

Sitting around the table were Shadow and Shrimp and Toon and Shakespeare and Stones, who today wore a snow-white eye patch with a narrow blood-red border.

Sunbeam looked at them all and wondered what Stones was smiling about.

"We need all you swinging dicks to get your duffle bags cleaned and your scissors sharpened," Sunbeam said, "and your sorry asses shifted into four-wheel drive. So listen up. Whoever the malevolent bastards are who're trying to move in on us, we need to teach them a lesson. A *harsh* lesson. We started last night, or you men did, and now we got to finish. We got to finish *fast*. Comments? Questions?" She sat leaning far forward in her chair with her elbows on the table. On the tabletop were two dead roaches in the green glass ashtray and her empty white coffee mug. With eyebrows raised Sunbeam looked hard at each man for two or three seconds.

They all looked back at her but no one said a word.

"Well?" she said.

"Any idea who these dudes are?" asked Shadow.

"I've heard rumors," Sunbeam answered. "We all know what rumors are worth. Dog shit. I heard they might be Mexicans. *Mexican* Mexicans. I also heard they might be Canadians. I even heard they might be a big-city gang from someplace down south. What I know almost for sure is, they intend to rip us off and run us out. Whoever they are, they must figure to go big-time. They think we're useless hicks out here. That's what I think they think. What I surmise. So I already sent word to the Big Dude across the mountain. I asked him for a few reinforcements. We should get six men and they should be here by the middle of this afternoon. They'll help us out and then we'll owe them one. What we need now is some strategy. Sure, we can intimidate, especially with the Big Dude's help. We can kick some ass. But we sure as hell don't want to kill anybody. That's not our style, not unless it's self-defense. *Comprende?*" Sunbeam looked hard at everyone around the table. "What the hell are you smiling about, Stones?"

"Nothing," Stones said. "I was thinking about something is all." It was warm in the room and he rubbed the sweat off his forehead with the back of his hand and then ran the hand the other way across his mouth to wipe the smile away. "Six dudes from the Big Dude?" he said. "Including the Hulk?"

"Why wouldn't the Big Dude send the Hulk? Sure, the Hulk'll be here."

"He's one mean motherfucker!" Shadow said.

"You got that right!" Toon agreed. "You can say that again!"

"He's one mean motherfucker!" Shadow repeated.

Stones laughed and Shadow joined him.

Shakespeare sat there trying unsuccessfully to stop worrying over his Supercock problems and Toon still felt aggravation over the fact that he couldn't make his tattoo session and Shrimp couldn't get Rainbow out of his mind. For years he'd been attracted to her and he felt certain she was attracted back, but she was married to Uncle Sam so he'd never hit on her once even when he was buzzed from beer or pleasantly stoned on weed because he knew hitting on her would weigh him down with guilt. But maybe now it was finally time.

All the men at the table took occasional sips from their pints of ale or stout. Sunbeam had told them that one pint each was all they would get for now. When their problems were resolved and she hoped that would happen today, and if not today no later than tomorrow, then they could relax. When the outsiders were dispelled by whatever means it took to do the job then her men could come back to the Bird of Prey and celebrate with as much ale and stout and prime weed as they wanted. Then they could seriously party with everything on her.

"Where *are* these outsider motherfuckers?" Shadow said and then sipped from his pint and slowly lowered the glass. "That's what we need to know, right? I mean, right now while we talk, where *are* they? We can't have any strategy if we don't have some idea where the fuck they *are*. Am I right?" He lifted his glass for another sip and lowered it slowly. "Do I make sense? Do I?" He raised his glass to drink yet again and lowered it slowly again.

"They want our cannabis," Sunbeam said. "Then they want our land to grow their own product. Where are they? My guess is, they're out prowling around one of our grows right this minute, maybe the same one where you caught them yesterday. That's our biggest grow and they must know it. What should we do? That's what we have to figure out. The only serious question is—"

They all heard tires squeal as a vehicle turned off the road at high speed into the parking lot. Two seconds after that the tires screeched on asphalt as the vehicle came to a quick stop outside the front door. The motor died and a door slammed shut hard and the front door of the tavern swung open and Deputy Winter stepped into the room. In his tight-fitting uniform he stood there short and fat and outlined against the bright outside light with his pig eyes squinted against the interior dimness. His silhouette included the .45 automatic and the nightstick and the Taser in the black leather holsters on his gun belt.

A faint smell of exhaust and burnt rubber drifted into the room.

"We're back here, lard ass," Sunbeam said and all the men at the table laughed quietly.

Winter leaned forward at the waist and squinted and saw them and then reached back to close the door.

He sauntered across the room to the table with the .45 bouncing up and down against the tube of fat where his hip should have been. There were no empty chairs so he stood behind Stones looking down at Sunbeam. "I'll lard ass you, you scrawny old bitch," he said with a forced smile. "But why's it so goddamn dark in here? Why's it like a goddamn haunted house?"

"We're environmentalists," Sunbeam answered. "We're conserving energy. We're fighting climate change and we're helping save the world from morons like you. Any objections? The point is, these trespassing outsider sons of bitches, these bastards, these rippers, want to come in here with pesticides and fertilizers. They want to drain the creeks dry and cut the big trees down. Not to mention the fact they want to rip us off. What about that?"

Winter opened his eyes wide and maintained his smile. "Well I'm here to help save your alls' sorry asses. You think I want outsiders around? All I want is to help you citizens out. Any objection to *that*?"

Stones had never liked Winter or trusted him and he began softly singing an old Bob Marley tune with slightly revised lyrics:

"I shot the sheriff, but I should have shot the deputy."

Shadow didn't like Winter either and he knew that in the old days the original hippies had called cops "pigs" and he threw his head back and conspicuously sniffed the air. "I do smell me some bacon," he said.

None of the young men around the table had ever liked Winter and they liked him less than ever now because they had all heard he intended to run for county commissioner and they all believed that politics was an even lower calling than law enforcement.

Winter ignored them all and went on talking. "You been compensating me for a good long time now, Sunbeam. In return I keep you informed. Ain't that it? It's been a good system, good relationship, works out just fine for everybody involved. We aim to keep our system going along good as ever and that's all. Ain't it, ol' girl?"

Sunbeam looked at everyone around the table and winked and smiled. "I guess we got just a little bit of time for some euphemisms now," she said. "'Compensating?'" she began, looking back at Winter. "You mean we've been bribing your fat ass, paying you off. 'Keeping us informed?' What you mean is, you've been ratting out the people you work for to get your bribes from us. You *are* ready to get into politics, Winter. Once you get elected you could call torture 'enhanced interrogation.' You could call planking your mistress 'hiking a trail.'"

"Euphemisms" was a game they played often and knew well and Shadow took the next turn: "Yeah, put ol' Winter here in politics and he can give a big speech about a war and call dead civilians 'collateral damage.' Or he could call bombing the civilians 'air support.'"

They worked their way around the table. "He could call his prisoners 'detainees,'" Shrimp said. "He could call shooting his buddies 'friendly fire.'"

Then came Toon: "When he wanted to get it from the dude in the toilet stall next door he could call it 'taking a wide stance.'"

"Or," Shakespeare said, "he could call bombing homes and killing innocent women and kids 'pacification.'"

"Or," Stones added, "if he got caught lying his fat ass off he could just say he 'misspoke.' Or he could—"

The detonation came like an unforeseen clap of thunder and the building shook and windows shattered behind the closed shutters, and powdery dust wafted from the walls and ceiling.

Shrimp sprinted across the room to the nearest window and threw the shutters wide and as shards of broken glass fell at his feet he squinted and blinked against the sunlight. The first thing he saw was a brown-gray cloud of dust and smoke and then within the quickly spreading and thinning cloud he saw Shakespeare's Bronco with its roof crushed nearly flat under the weight of one of the metal stanchions that had fallen. The stanchion lay across the Bronco and extended all the way across the road. The second stanchion lay parallel to the road and the Bird of Prey sign had come down bent and misshapen on the shoulder of the road between the stanchions.

When he looked down south Shrimp saw a shiny gray pickup he thought might be a Dodge Ram traveling fast and by then the others had crowded around the window to look.

"My Bronco!" Shakespeare said. "My fucking Bronco! *Look* at that motherfucker! What the fuck happened?"

"A goddamn explosion happened!" Winter said.

"No shit, Sherlock!" Sunbeam said.

"Don't get wise!" Winter answered.

"Who the fuck did it?" Shakespeare said.

"Who the fuck knows?" Winter answered.

Though he stood in warm sunlight Shrimp suddenly felt like a bare-chested man in icy wind with nothing to wear against the cold and he turned quickly and squirmed through the small crowd and crossed the room and took the stairs two at a time and opened Rainbow's door without knocking and there she was sitting on the chair beside Uncle Sam's bed. Smoke and dust that had blown into the room through the shattered window behind the bed coated everything.

"What happened?" Rainbow asked without looking up. "What was it?"

"No idea," Shrimp said. "Are you all right? Is Uncle Sam?"

"When the window busted open some glass landed on the bed. But I already cleaned it off, he's all right. We were lucky. None of it hit his face. He didn't get cut any. I was back in the bathroom when it happened." Rainbow was stroking Uncle Sam's forehead. "When I told him I loved him after it happened he blinked his eyes," she said. "It even looked like he tried to talk. It did."

"Listen! Listen to me now! Are you sure you're all right?"

"We're all right. Yes we are. Are you? Is everybody else?"

"Yes."

"But what's happening? What should we do?"

"Stay where you are. Just stay right here for now. I'll be back in a while, I promise. Are you sure you're okay?"

"Yes!"

Back downstairs the small crowd remained clustered near the window. Inside the tavern the dust had settled and outside the smoke had drifted off in the late morning breeze.

When he reached the window Shrimp saw that two south-bound cars and a northbound log truck had already been stopped on the road by the fallen stanchion. Two elderly couples on one side of the stanchion and the short burly man who had to be the log truck driver on the other side were standing there talking.

Winter stood with his back to the window facing the others. Shrimp had heard Winter talking on his way down the stairs and he thought Winter sounded like many men of authority he'd seen and heard who always acted sure of themselves but seldom made sense.

"We get these disturbances often enough," Winter was saying now, "pretty damn often, maybe not this extreme but extreme enough, and you can't panic, oh no, not that, because the only way to make sure you don't panic is not to let yourself, understand me? Sure you do! Things ain't always as bad as they seem! Sometimes they're worse! Some sorry sons of bitches did this shit because they panicked but we won't, not me!"

"Goddamn it, fatso," Sunbeam said. "Cut the bullshit!"

"See? That right there's panic talking! We got to cool off an' *think,* figure things! We got to—"

"I said cut the shit, fatso! You're a useless asshole, a piece of shit, a turd!"

"I'll forget you said that, Sunbeam," Winter answered, "because it wasn't *you* who said it!"

"It sure as hell was!"

"I'll forget because that was *fear* talkin', woman! An explosion gets to people! Oh, I know explosions! You got to get *hold* of yourself now, *all* of you do, we got to—"

"You fat son of a bitchin' asshole!" Toon interrupted. "Who the fuck you figure you're talkin' to? Us guys in here've been in way more explosions than you could fuckin' *count!*"

"You got to get hold of yourself now, *all* of you do, we got to—"

Winter broke it off when the motorists stopped on the road walked through the front door with the log truck driver leading the way and the elderly couples following close behind him.

The log truck driver was pot-bellied and middle-aged and wearing faded jeans and a plaid shirt with the sleeves rolled up to the elbows. He wore wire-rimmed glasses and his long black hair was tied into a ponytail. As he passed through the door he pulled the tail of his shirt out of his jeans and used it to clean his glasses. After replacing his glasses and tucking his shirt back in he finally spoke, "Who in hell knocked down that pole out there?" he asked the room. "Or what in hell? How the hell'd that happen? What's goin' on around here?"

"We been wonderin' the same damn thing ourselves," answered Winter. "It ain't been down more'n ten minutes."

"Well I got me a load of Doug fir I got to get delivered," said the driver. "What in hell you intend to do?"

"What I'm gonna do is," Winter answered, "I'm gonna tell you to get on back out there an' chain up your rig to that pole an' then put 'er in reverse an' drag that sucker off an' clear the road. You do that an' you can deliver that Doug fir any damn place you want." Winter looked at the two elderly couples and smiled and nodded at them. "An' these fine citizens here," he said, "they can go on about their business too once you get that pole dragged off."

At that one of the old ladies spoke up: "Melvin and me are headed to a birthday party! My sister's eighty-eight years old tomorrow! She's miles down yonder in the nursing home! Garden of Eden. That's what they call that nursing home."

"Okay, I'll do 'er!" the log truck driver said. "I can do 'er! An' then after I do 'er I'm marchin' straight back in here for a quick cold one!"

"Olive, that's my sister, she's got the Alzheimer's," said the old woman, "but she's A-okay except for that! She just can't remember stuff an' can't think is all! My name's Olivia! Olive and Olivia! That was us! Still is!"

"We better help that dude get his truck hitched up," said Shadow.

All the men walked single-file out the door.

"Olive, she can't remember who we are, but we'll be there! Once that pole gets off the road that is! I never did like poles that much!"

"Will you pipe down, Olivia?" said Melvin. "Will you stuff a cork in it?"

The other couple—a tall old man with a shiny wooden cane and a skinny lady with white hair tied into a high bun—stood still with their heads down and remained silent.

"You all sit down now," Sunbeam told them. "You folks take seats anywhere you want. I doubt if it'll take long, but you might as well relax while you're waiting."

The couples took the table nearest the open door and turned their chairs so they could sit and watch what was happening outside.

Winter gestured to Sunbeam with his fat white hand. "Now that we got a few minutes, let's you an' me sit down and talk one more time in private," he said.

Sunbeam followed him toward the back of the room.

They sat at the table as far away as they could get from the old couples up front.

"One question," Winter began. "I'm curious is all. Are you satisfied with the way I play dumb? Am I still convincing enough?"

"Oh yes," Sunbeam answered. "I have to admit you keep getting better all the time. You even have me fooled about half the time. I guess you just must be a born natural."

"Your gratuitous insults don't impress me. Never did. Have you ever read *Huckleberry Finn*?"

"A long time ago I did, in school. Sure. Doesn't everybody?"

"Then you must remember the King and Duke."

"Those con men."

"One of them, I think it was the Duke, plays what they call 'the deaf and dumb' when they're trying to swindle a family out of their rightful inheritance. That's somewhere toward the end of the story. That scene functions as a kind of inspiration to me. But they'll get that stanchion dragged off pronto so let's get to the point and make this quick. Things have changed some. Things have changed considerably. Last night final orders came in from upstairs, from the top dog."

"And?"

"So just listen. We're well on our way toward providing ourselves extremely comfortable and satisfying lives. There's big money waiting for us. Playing an idiot and dealing with you is the small price I've been obliged to pay. The point is, things are about to get better than ever, for us, and I hope I'm safe in assuming you want that to happen as much as I do. Am I correct?"

The expression on Sunbeam's tanned face was that of an impatient woman waiting for a bus already fifteen or twenty minutes late. After a few seconds she nodded and then she did her best to smile.

"Good," Winter said. "Things are moving fast. Everything is right on schedule, including that accident out there on the road." As he spoke he nodded toward the front of the building. "Later today my new business partners, your partners too whether you like it or not, have arranged for their contingent of foot soldiers to arrive at the big grow where the trouble was yesterday. They'll spread out from there. All the people they need, more than they need, are here and fully prepared. They came up over Baldy Mountain on the old one-way gravel road, armed and dangerous. So I need to relay some fresh news to you. Unwelcome news no doubt. Your boys, some of them, at least a few of them, might be in some serious trouble."

"What? How serious?"

"Serious," Winter said. "Possibly life-threatening serious. It's not in my hands. I can't help it. Nobody can."

"We have reinforcements coming in from the Big Dude."

"But the Big Dude's not that big in the big picture. Crazy Carlos's people should get here about the same time your boys do, and I suppose about the same time the Big Dude and his boys do too. You got to get your boys over to that grow as fast as you can. The top dog's people have plans to rip out every plant and carry it all away by the end of the week. They know where all the grows are. They don't just know where they are, they have them mapped out in detail. I'd say they have better maps than the Forest Service ever did. They'll move through the grows one by one, day by day."

"Then I won't send my boys out there. No. Are you crazy? No way!"

"Listen now! One more time. Just listen up! You're not the boss here and neither am I! These orders, our orders, are coming from very high up. It's a long, complicated chain of command. If you and I don't do as we're told, *we* might die. If we tried to run away they'd get us. If we tried to just give them everything they want and head off into the sunset they'd very likely kill us anyway. We know too much. Way too much. The point is, we'd be examples to everybody everywhere. We have to do what these people say, no matter how crazy it is. These people operate through intimidation. They *enjoy* killing people. *Nobody* crosses them. *Nobody* says no or even maybe to them. It's that crazy. It's that simple. They send harsh messages to anybody who might ever *dream* about crossing them. *You* have to understand. Because you're in this now the same way I am and it's way too late to back out unless *you* want to die. Understand?"

"You never told me this shit before," Sunbeam said. "You never told me anywhere along the line. You never told me *anything* like this would happen."

Winter stared hard at her. "In case you're interested," he said, "I'll tell you what your major malfunction is, what it's been all along. Old as you are, you still have the mind of a hippie, and as far as I can tell most of your boys, likely due to your influence, are pretty much the same way most of the time. Sure, they can kick some gluteus maximus when they know they have to, when there's no other option. But generally they'd prefer to just drift along. Trust in luck. Let things happen. Well, the truth may well be that you've all used too much of your own product for too long, and this time you've drifted too far. *I* can't do anything about it now. It's not *my* fault. Accept the fact. That's the way it is."

Sunbeam wondered how much Winter had known and how long he had known it. All she knew for certain was that he'd never cared about anyone but himself. She stared back at his fat face and wondered how it had come so far. How had *she* come so far? Everything had sounded simple at first and the plans kept changing and things kept getting worse and the snowball had rolled down a steep hill growing fast and picking up speed and now here she was powerless at the bottom of the hill. First she felt frightened and then angry and then sick.

"This is bullshit!" she said.

"It may be bullshit," Winter answered, "but people above us changed the rules."

Sunbeam heard the sounds of clanking chains and then the log truck roaring to life.

She remembered the time she'd been chained up and hauled off to jail in San Francisco. She and her blue-eyed friend Cornflower had marched in the front row of a protest against the war and they had blocked traffic at Union Square near the St. Francis Hotel and the entire front row had been arrested and twelve young women were chained together by mean cops and herded into a van and driven to jail. The back of the van smelled of sweat and pot and exhaust fumes and she and Cornflower began a song and soon everyone was singing along and they sang all the way to jail. They were locked in cells for the night and they sang all night and they were released after first light in the morning and they sang as they left the city jail.

Sunbeam had been happy then and now for the first time in her life she hated herself. She hated what she had done and what she had become and most of all she hated the fact that there was nothing she could do about any of it. She looked at the floor. She stared at the white string from a mop caught under a front leg of her chair.

"This is awful," she said. "Fucking awful."

"Even if we tried to run off they'd get us. I *know* that. It's the truth. But try to look at it this way. We're all set. It's dog eat dog and we're in with the biggest dogs. The biggest dogs might be crazy but our payoff'll be huge." Winter looked over Sunbeam's shoulder. "The road must be clear out there. Here they come back. You just make sure you get your boys where they need to be in a hurry. Make sure they're there soon. You *have* to. Understand?"

"*Beer!*" the log truck driver called from up front. "*Beer I said beer I said beer! I need me a cold one cold one cold one! Yes!*"

ONE WAY ROAD

When Shrimp hurried back upstairs to check in with Rainbow he found her sitting in bright sunlight close beside Uncle Sam's bed. She was looking out the window as she stroked his hair.

"I was watching you guys drag that thing off the road," she said without looking around when she heard Shrimp come into the room. "You made it look so easy."

"That log truck driver knows his stuff. Good man. You sure everything's okay up here?"

"Oh yes."

"You figure Uncle Sam knows what happened? You figure he knows anything happened? You think he heard the explosion?"

"I don't know. Maybe. I think he hears us, sometimes at least. I even think he wants to talk to us and almost can. Maybe he will someday. You want to talk to him? Want to spell me a while?"

"We're taking off in ten minutes. We got business to attend to. I can talk to him till then."

Rainbow stood up from her chair and kissed Shrimp's cheek and held his hand briefly and squeezed it and Shrimp squeezed her hand back and took her place on the chair.

He looked down at Uncle Sam. "Hey, buddy," he said. He looked into Uncle Sam's eyes and studied his face carefully. Over the months and years Uncle Sam never seemed to change but Shrimp thought that might be because he saw him too often to notice the changes. When he'd come home from war he'd been shocked at how his parents had aged but he understood it was because he hadn't seen them in more than three years.

"You're lookin' okay, dude," he said to Uncle Sam. When he talked to Uncle Sam with Rainbow in the room he wasn't certain which one he was actually talking to. He could feel Rainbow standing behind him now and supposed he might be talking to them both.

Down on the road the old couples had climbed slowly into their cars and now they were heading south with the two old men driving. The lead car was a red Ford sedan and the second car was a blue Volkswagen sedan. The log truck was already out of sight.

Then two identical black Cadillac Escalades with dark-tinted windows came speeding north no more than twenty feet apart and they slowed some as they passed the tavern and then resumed their high speed and soon disappeared around the bend beyond the Jump Off Joe Creek Bridge.

"Did you see that?" Rainbow said.

"Uninvited guests," Shrimp answered. "You're lookin' okay, dude," he repeated to Uncle Sam. "Hell, the truth is you're lookin' better than me. I been missing out on my beauty sleep lately. Busy time of year. Two big ol' four-wheel boats roared by outside just now. What the fuck's that all about? Like I said, uninvited guests. Scumbags usually have the best vehicles, right?"

Shrimp could still feel Rainbow standing behind him and still feel the place on his cheek where she had kissed him. "I guess we got a little war coming up right out here in the woods, in the sticks. How come people call the country 'the sticks'? 'Cause of the trees? Trees ain't sticks, are they? I still get the nightmares with the sweats sometimes. I did last night. I sure hope you don't get the nightmares, buddy. Remember ol' Cowboy? He was in my nightmare. Sure you remember ol' Cowboy. He was only with the outfit a week or two but you guys rode the same vehicle. Remember what his real name was? I'm pretty sure it was Horace Jones the Third. The *Third*! Judging by that one, we knew, one Jones, one Cowboy, would've been enough. *More* than enough. Who the hell needed three? I sure as shit hope the first two Joneses were better than that douche bag we ended up with. He stole your cigarettes, I remember that. Right out of your footlocker. Then after he stole your cigarettes he swiped your hash. They never found much of him that morning after the blast. Lucky you weren't sittin' next to him that day. We never scraped up much of him off that street. That's what my nightmare was about, the mess we scraped up. Hell, they could've shipped him home in his footlocker, easy. They could've shipped him home in a bucket with a lid. Jones the Third came from someplace in Oklahoma. Ever been to Oklahoma? I was there for eight solid weeks, Fort Sill, Lawton, Oklahoma. Artillery school. We learned to fire 105 howitzers and once we left Fort Sill I never saw a 105 again. I shouldn't maybe be so tough on ol' Jones number three. From all I saw there Oklahoma's no place you want to come from. Or go to either. Too bad we can't pick where we come from and go to. Ain't that the truth?"

Shrimp looked hard at Uncle Sam and felt Rainbow standing close behind him and thought he should stop talking but didn't.

GROWER'S MARKET

"I'd pray for you, buddy, if I thought it made any sense," he said. "If I figured there was some kind of god who might listen to me. You listen now, I got to go here pretty quick. Sunbeam's sendin' us out to work. Sunbeam an' that asshole deputy."

FIRST ESCALADE DRIVER

As always he felt relaxed and confident driving the lead Cadillac along the rural road through country he had never seen before and doubted he would ever see again. For eighteen of the thirty-one years of his life driving had been his livelihood. In the early years it was expensive cars stolen late at night and driven across the border before morning. He was barely fourteen when a jefe from a drug cartel bought him from the jefe who sold the stolen cars. When he tried to escape and got caught the beating he took resulted in six broken ribs and broken bones in both legs and seven teeth knocked out of his mouth with a quart Tecate beer bottle. As soon as he was sufficiently healed he tried to escape again and was caught and beaten again and then raped by many men. Not long after that the cartel was battling another cartel for control of a large and lucrative territory. Five men from the rival cartel were captured at a nightclub and taken by van to a lonely desert canyon many miles from the nearest village. He was the driver. The prisoners were held at gunpoint and four of them were stripped except for T-shirts, and then gasoline from a five-gallon red plastic container was poured over their heads and he was given the job of lighting and tossing the matches. The gasoline ignited with loud huffs of air and the men with the pistols stood together and shot the four burning screaming writhing victims to death and made jokes and laughed while they did it. When they drove away from that place after the shootings they left the fifth prisoner there so he could tell his people what had happened. An hour away on a lonely beach the men drank Hornitos tequila from bottles they had brought from the nightclub. They let him drink too and he had been a cartel driver ever since.

SECOND ESCALADE DRIVER

He was saving money that would give him time to paint. At age eighteen he had been arrested for possession and sale of marijuana. His pornographic drawings had been widely admired through school and as a way to pass time in the state prison he took up painting with oils and acrylics. From the very start people who saw his work knew he had talent and he loved painting landscapes and portraits. Shortly before he was granted parole he won an art fellowship to a prestigious and progressive university but he had no intention of attending school. He wanted to paint and that was all. The first thing he did upon arrival at the university was claim a check in his name at the financial aid office to cover a semester's expenses. He walked to a nearby bank and cashed the check and bought a good used car at a lot two blocks away and then late in the rainy afternoon he visited the university art gallery. It was still raining late that night when he broke into the gallery and stole six valuable paintings. He cut the paintings from elaborate frames with a razor blade and rolled them up and carried them out and had driven them four hundred miles before the theft was discovered. Seven hundred miles away he tried to sell the paintings but was arrested and jailed and returned to a prison. This second prison didn't allow him to paint and now he was on parole again and his plan was to save money until he had enough to buy his own new car and drive it to a small town on the Pacific coast of Costa Rica that a cellmate had described for him in great and loving detail. The town was Manuel Antonio and once he arrived he would buy a house and set up his studio and paint. He calculated he was no more than three or four months from living his dream.

* * *

Case parked at the trailhead and bushwhacked half a mile through the forest and then climbed a steep slope and set out hiking along the west ridge to reach yesterday's grow. In his spare backpack he carried two quart containers of water and two red apples and several strips of venison jerky and a Swiss army knife and half a dozen .20 gauge shotgun shells. The shells held number 6 shot, which was what he had always used for upland hunting. In his good right hand he carried his Winchester over and under. He thought he might break tradition and kill a blue grouse if he had a sure shot but not a ruffed grouse because their local populations were thinning for unknown reasons.

The valley was miles from any road or established trail. Fifty years ago a reservoir had been formed when the main branch of Jump Off Joe Creek was dammed and the water behind the dam had isolated the valley. A family named Tucker had established a homestead in the valley in the spring of 1881 and three generations of Tuckers lived and died there and were buried there before the dam was built. Since the dam had gone in, no one knew of any Tuckers anywhere.

Jump Off Joe Creek's east branch cut the valley almost exactly in half with steep wooded mountains on three sides and then the massive stone wall of the reservoir at the bottom end. At the top of the valley where the creek spilled over a solid rock waterfall there were signs of an Indian encampment for people who knew how to look for signs. Flakes and chips of obsidian lay buried beneath leaves and pine needles and there were occasional arrowheads and spear points and scrapers to be found along the creek banks after the high water of spring runoff. Faintly discernible pictographs were etched into the rock walls on the very upper reaches of the creek.

After discovering the pictographs Case had climbed the rock walls to explore the four small caves there. Inside the caves he came upon mortars and pestles and a quiver with five arrows in it. The arrow shafts had bird points, which proved men had hunted grouse in the valley long ago. In the most difficult cave to reach were three human skeletons. They were two adults with a child between them and all of them lay on their backs side by side. Case hadn't taken anything from the cave. He hadn't touched anything. The stone ceilings were black from the smoke of cooking fires. The natives had used the caves in wintertime and during bad weather. They had lived on fish and game and lasted many centuries longer than the Tuckers.

Black oaks along with poison oak and a few pines and willow thickets grew along both creek banks with open ground between the vegetation and the mountains on either side. The marijuana grow was situated on the open ground on both sides of the creek and stretched nearly the length of the valley.

Case limped along and finally crested the last small rise and stood at the high point on the ridge with the long valley stretching toward the reservoir far below him. He wore a short-sleeved shirt and his right forearm was bandaged and he used the heel of his left hand to press the tape at both edges of the dressing but because he was sweating it wouldn't stick. It was no more than yet another injury and one more minor pain. Many years ago before he had been a soldier himself Case had read a novel about soldiers and war. He couldn't recall the title but now he remembered a scene in which an enlisted man had regarded his body's scars as a book about his life.

Standing on top of the hill Case tried to mentally list all the wounds and scars and healed bones that comprised the pages of his own life. Beginning at the top there was a long scar that reached from just below his right ear to the middle of his throat. His right arm had been fractured in three places and his left arm in two. Two bones in his right hand had been broken in the same explosion. There were scars on his back and his chest and both thighs. His knee had been operated on and then eight months later operated on again to correct the mistakes made in the first surgery. He realized he'd almost forgotten his mangled wrist even though he could barely close his left hand all the way into a fist.

Directly across the valley from where he stood a small flock of band-tailed pigeons fluttered out of one tall fir and then flew fifty yards and settled into the top limbs of another fir. Seeing the band-tails made him momentarily happy. They were the first flock he had seen in this country in years. Like so many wild species the band-tails were gradually disappearing.

He had brought Heather here before there was a grow and they had always enjoyed visiting the Tucker cabin that sat near the middle of the valley. The day they first happened onto the place was in the spring and standing up high where he stood today they had looked down on a valley filled with thick white fog looking like rich milk filling a bowl.

Then as they hiked downhill the fog burned away under the late morning sun and soon they discovered the cabin with white and yellow daffodils blooming profusely between the well house and the front door. When they poked around inside Case found kitchen drawers lined with brittle newspaper pages with stories about Herbert Hoover and Babe Ruth. There were charred chunks of wood in the cookstove. Mason jars of preserves and tomatoes and green beans were lined up on a warped plank shelf above the tarnished metal sink. The glass jars had turned opaque with age. Shelves below the preserves held pots and pans and plates and dishes and empty jars. The steep narrow stairway to the second floor was solidly intact and they climbed carefully with Case leading the way.

In the second floor bedroom a gray long-sleeved dress that had once been white lay over the back of a wooden rocking chair beside rusted bedsprings on a crude wooden frame. A wooden frame without a picture in it hung on a nail in the wall over the bedsprings. Close to the empty picture frame a wide-brimmed straw hat hung on a wooden peg. Case tried the hat on but it was too small and he hung it back on the peg. Under the springs sat a cracked pair of men's leather boots without laces.

Outside behind the cabin they came upon an old plow and the head of a splitting axe driven into a chopping block and leather harnesses and horseshoes and a child's tricycle and countless rusted cans and empty bottles. Some of the bottles were clear glass and some blue and some green and a few of the small green bottles had Chinese writing on them. Case thought they were medicine bottles. He and Heather guessed at what the Tuckers might have been like and speculated about the kind of lives they'd lived.

Now after all these years the daffodils were gone and the cabin had collapsed into a pile of logs and splintered beams piled around the stone chimney and Case was here alone.

"Heather," he said.

Then Case glimpsed the flash across the valley in the shade underneath the fir tree the band-tails had abandoned and less than a half second later the .30 caliber bullet tore through his chest. He never heard the sound that arrived after the bullet. The impact knocked him backward but not off his feet and the second bullet that he never heard passed through his right shoulder and spun him around and he fell flat on his face.

He lay there dazed and remembering. The last time he'd been shot long ago there had been no pain and now there wasn't any either. Just like the other time the bullets had hit like hard blows from a fist or a hammer or the kick of a horse. Now he had gone numb all over and his head seemed weightless. With his face in the dirt and his arms at his sides he remembered his left wrist and tried to clench the hand into a fist but couldn't tell whether or not he'd done it. As it had long ago the warm blood in his mouth tasted salty. He could hear himself breathing and could hear his heart pumping but had no sense of time and he tried to count off his breaths but he couldn't make it past three. After he stopped trying to count was when he heard footsteps.

He wanted to roll over but couldn't. He couldn't move and a great weightlessness seemed to fill him now.

When the footsteps stopped he heard voices.

"Is he dead?"

"Naw. Can't you see him breathin'?"

"Finish him then."

"What the fuck for? Look at 'im. I mean look at what's left. He'll croak soon enough. Relax."

Yes this was the end and he'd always feared the end would come in a hospital bed with tubes and needles and plastic bags and doctors and nurses pretending they cared but he'd also always been lucky and he thought he was lucky now. He was ready. Yes. The best luck of all had been Heather at the very start when he'd smiled at a stranger at a boring party and she smiled back and her look said save me from this place and he did. He'd have smiled at the memory now if he could as he lay in the dirt dying. He heard himself say Heather in his mind.

"Who is he?"

"He's an old dead dude. Almost dead dude that is. Soon to be dead dude, right? Relax. We'll stay right up here anyway right up till our guests arrive."

"You think we should?"

"*I know we should. We're supposed to. It's all worked out. We'll finish up everything this afternoon.*"

"*Why'd you shoot him?*"

"*I do what I'm told. Anyway that's what the government trained me for. I'm good at it. Good as anybody. I got a very sweet weapon here. Got to use the weapon. Got to utilize it to its full potential.*"

"*I hear you. Awesome weapon. But hey. I hear that old bitch at the tavern is a weird one.*"

"*Weird?*"

"*Weird.*"

"*She's cool.*"

"*Whitey said she weirded him out.*"

"*Sometimes Whitey weirds me out. The bitch is cool. She got everything worked out. She's okay.*"

"*Okay, okay.*"

"*Sure you got enough blasting caps?*"

"*More than enough, dude.*"

"*This dude right here's dead already, see? He's the first.*"

"*But not the last. Should we bury the son of a bitch?*"

"*What for? Why bother? It doesn't matter what happens to anybody after they're dead.*"

"*Well at least we should drag him back in the woods. You want his gun?*"

"*That peashooter? The dude's not fat. You drag him. See what he's got on him first.*"

"*Jesus, that's a fucking lot of blood.*"

"*We're used to it, right?*"

"*To what?*"

"Blood."

"Yeah I guess."

"Go on then."

"Hey, man! In his backpack! Jerky!"

"Cool!"

COMMERCE

With Deputy Winter gone Sunbeam sat with her young men gathered around her table. Her hand trembled as she sketched out the valley with a ballpoint pen on the top sheet of a pad of lined yellow paper.

She printed names at each landmark on the map.

"You okay?" Stones asked her.

She nodded her head and said, "Hell yes!" but didn't look up.

"You crying?" Stones asked her.

"Hell no!" she said.

Sunbeam tore off the map and pushed it across the table to Shadow.

"You boys go on now," she said. "Get!"

As they stood up and then walked off she pretended to write notes on the blank sheet at the top of her pad.

After they walked out the front door the Bird of Prey was empty.

Sunbeam stood and hurried across the room to the window.

She watched her boys drive off all together in Stones's muddy Subaru.

As the Subaru rounded the bend at Jump Off Joe she waved.

She walked back to her table and sat alone drinking strong black coffee and smoking a fresh joint. She didn't think the joint would help and it didn't. She thought about going after her men and warning them off but she knew Winter had told her the truth. He was a fat greedy evil son of a bitch but he always told the truth about things when money was involved. But she wondered if he'd known about the top dog's plans all along. Her boys were seasoned by combat and tough and mean when they had to be and she hoped it would help them now but knew it probably wouldn't. All odds were heavily stacked against them. It was too late to find a way out or to change what she feared might happen.

Sunbeam remembered her early years in this peaceful country. She and all her friends were naïve about nearly everything they needed to know to survive in an untamed place but somehow they had struggled and learned and established decent lives for themselves. They had all loved the trout streams and the wooded hills and the wild birds and animals and the fresh winter snow and the vivid colors of wildflowers against lush green grass after the snow melted in spring.

Every April Sunbeam had loved walking naked through green grass and wildflowers to swim in Jump Off Joe Creek with the water running high and hard and icy cold with snowmelt. Then she was young and strong and full of hope and now she felt as useless as a puppet with its strings cut.

Rainbow came quietly through the door from upstairs and walked across the room and took a chair at the table.

"What's wrong?" she asked Sunbeam.

"I'd leave this place if I was you," Sunbeam answered.

"Why?"

"I just would. I'll give you all the money you need."

"I have money."

"You and Uncle Sam ought to go someplace else."

"I've saved up plenty of money, thanks to you. Enough to last a long time."

"You still think you might become a nurse someday?"

"I'd like to." Rainbow nodded her head and smiled. "I want to try. What I'm thinking is, I can get care for Uncle Sam while I'm in school and then afterwards too. I mean, I'll care for him, always, as long as he lives. In school I'd learn stuff that could help me do a better job with him. But, yes, I'd love being a real nurse."

"Well now's as good a time as any. You'd be a fine nurse. You should go on and leave. This lonely country out here's changed. Changed plenty. You find yourself a nice town with a school with the program you need and settle there. There's nursing schools all over. Everybody needs nurses. They always will. How's your van running these days?"

"Running just fine. Shrimp works on the van whenever it needs repairs. Two weeks ago he put in a fuel pump."

"I got chained up and crammed into a van once."

"Chained up? Really?"

"Arrested at an antiwar protest down in San Francisco. The old days."

"What's wrong with you, Sunbeam? How come you're crying? What's the matter?"

"Honey, the old days are gone."

GROWER'S MARKET

* * *

By shortly after noon Sunbeam's men had reached their scattered locations bordering the big grow. She had stationed Shadow and Shrimp just below the waterfall that fed into the valley. With their loaded weapons cradled in their laps and wearing faded army fatigue pants and long-sleeved camouflage T-shirts they sat leaning back against a smooth gray boulder in the shade of a giant sugar pine. Big cones that had fallen from limbs high in the tree lay scattered all around them on the forest floor. They watched what they could see of the grow and the open country down the valley toward the reservoir.

On the ground between them in an old Kelty backpack were spare magazines of ammo and a set of Bushnell quick-focusing hunting binoculars and six salami sandwiches and two packs of Pall Mall cigarettes and an old souvenir Zippo lighter and two quarts of water and four brown pint bottles of oatmeal stout. They had snuck the stout out of the Bird of Prey while Sunbeam wasn't looking. They could hear the sound of the falls from where they sat and both men drank stout and smoked Pall Malls as they watched the country and talked to pass the time.

They believed they were in a safe and secure place for now and were well into their first bottles when Shadow posed an old question: "What the fuck are we *doing* here? Explain it to me. I mean, tell me why we're right here, right now, today."

"Right now we're doing what the fuck we like," Shrimp answered. "Sipping some brews. Sitting on our asses. Bullshitting.

Trying to figure things out. This could maybe be another fucking false alarm."

"Maybe. Maybe not. We *never* know what's happening. That's our problem. Like our restaurant we figure to open some day. When's it going to be? Where's it going to be? *What's* it going to be. We talk about it. We argue about it. But we never figure that out or anything else out either. Do we?"

"No. I guess not. Not really. But we'll figure it out about the restaurant. It's an important thing but not a *big* thing. Not *really* big I mean. It's the *really* big things that count most. Who the fuck ever figures them out?"

"Big things like what?"

"Like what the world's really all about," Shrimp said. "Like why the fuck people are like they are. Like why Uncle Sam ended up like he did. Like why shit always gets worse instead of better. Who figures that out?"

"Somebody must."

"Who?"

"Don't ask me. But if nobody ever figures anything like that out then we're all idiots for trying. Right?"

Shrimp smiled and sipped some stout. "More like morons," he said. "At least we *know* we're morons. It's the people who don't even know they're morons who're the *real* fucking morons. Or they're idiots. That's how I see it. Most of the time."

"Yeah, well what about the rest of the time? Explain to me how you see it then."

"I guess I don't worry about it the rest of the time. Worry too much and you end up going nuts. Hey, dude, how's your head?"

"My headache's about gone," Shadow said. "Ninety percent gone. At least ninety. The stitches feel okay too. I always did heal fast. Charity says my head looks like a football though."

"Looks more like a split coconut to me."

"I felt like shit this morning but no *problema* now." Shadow snubbed his cigarette out on the sole of his boot. "But what gets me is, sometimes it's like we're still enlisted men. I mean, here we are waiting around with weapons for assholes we never even met. Maybe they're not even assholes. For all we know maybe they're nice guys."

Shrimp looked up and pointed where a plane that appeared as a barely visible shining silver speck was leaving a long white jet trail thin as a hair across a blue and cloudless sky. "You ever wonder who's in those high-flying planes?" he said. "Looks like that baby's headed up north over the pole. London maybe. Or Frankfurt or Zurich. Paris. Rome. It's all filled up with people we never met and we don't give a shit about them and they don't give a shit about us. So what? What difference does it make?"

"At least we know the people on the plane exist," Shrimp said. "Maybe that drink cart's rattling down the aisle right now. Some hot flight attendant handing out cocktails or whatever. Vodka and tonics. Screwdrivers. Irish coffees. I could use an Irish coffee about now. This warm stout almost sucks."

"Nobody serves Irish coffees on planes. And if you were on a plane and got to London and ordered a stout it'd be warm there too. And when was the last time you saw a hot flight attendant? Maybe they used to be hot about fifty years ago. That's what I heard anyway."

"I could use me a vodka and tonic then. A tequila sunrise. I bet they serve anything you want up in first class."

"We could afford first class if we wanted," Shadow said.

"Yeah, but I'd never feel at home up in first class. I'd never feel right chilling with all the rich assholes. Anyway, the food in first class sucks almost as much as the food in economy."

"It might be a little bit better."

"Not much."

"You got it right, not much. Maybe you get it on a plate instead of in some fucked up plastic tray is all."

"Hey, Shadow, you ever notice what Italian food they serve lots of times on planes?"

"Lasagna?"

"You got that right. You ever notice how bad it sucks? That's *Italian* food, that you claim is the best, and the lasagna they serve on those planes is the worst shit I ever tried to eat anywhere. If I was starving on the Sahara desert or the fucking North Pole I doubt if I could eat that shit. Am I right, dude?"

Shadow sat up and reached for another Pall Mall and lit it. "*All* airplane food sucks," he said. "If they served French food it would suck, if they served German food it would suck, and if they served Chinese food it would suck, and if they served Mexican food it would suck worse than anything." He exhaled a thin stream of smoke and shook his head and smiled.

"They'd be way better off serving Mexican food instead of lasagna," Shrimp said. "Tacos. Enchiladas. Burritos. Chicken Mole. Fajitas. Tamales. All I'm saying is, not some fucked up limp pasta mixed up with cheese and tomato sauce."

"They should serve pizza on planes," Shadow said. "Pizza's always good. Pizza's good anywhere."

"Oh yeah? You mean some goddamn stale loaf of bread that got run over by a steamroller and then some moron poured melted cheese and tomato sauce all over it?"

"I got a question for you. You remember that Mexican grocery store in town, where we stopped that time to pick up some beer?"

"Yeah, I remember."

"You remember the meat counter they had in that place?"

Shrimp shook his head no.

"Well I do," Shadow said. "It was fucking disgusting. They had brains on display behind the glass. Intestines stuffed into plastic bags. Lungs. Tongues. They even had balls I think."

"Balls?"

"Testicles. Bull nuts. If their food was really any good why would they eat that shit? I went surfing down in Costa Rice once, years ago it was. I went into some little joint one night to eat and I asked the waiter if they had any good soup. So the son of a bitch smiled and said yes and guess what he brought me? A bowl of soup with fucking eyeballs floating around in it. Fish eyeballs they were. That's disgusting."

"So tell me what the fuck Costa Rica has to do with Mexico."

"They speak Spanish there, that's what. So they eat the same kind of crap there as in Mexico."

"Yeah, well, you know why they eat that stuff? 'Cause they use all the parts from the animals they kill. Why's it disgusting? It makes total fucking sense. Study some history, man. Some culture. Don't bad-mouth the Mexicans. Listen. It's getting pretty goddamn hairy around these parts. So I figure we got to make our move fairly soon. What if we had a place with *both* kinds of food?"

"Italian and Mexican, both?"

"Why not?"

Shadow took half a minute to answer. He inhaled three deep drags from his Pall Mall and exhaled the smoke slowly as he thought. He ground out the short butt on the sole of his boot. Finally he nodded his head and turned to look Shrimp in the eye. "Okay. I hear you, man. I could live with that. Yeah, why not? We could call the place Italiano-Mexicano."

"Hold on, man. *Un momento.* Mexicano-Italiano sounds more like it to me."

"Yeah, well I figure alphabetical order works, just like the way they seated us in third grade."

This time Shrimp took time to think. "Okay," he said. "Italiano-Mexicano's good enough for me. We argued long enough. See? We finally figured something out. I got no idea how the fuck it happened but it did."

"How long you figure we'll be out here?"

"You mean today?"

"Yeah, today."

"No idea."

"Want another stout?"

"Not yet," Shrimp said.

From nearby a pair of mourning doves began to call.

"Those dumb-ass doves should be gone south out of here by now," Shadow said.

"They'll be gone pretty soon. Anyway, back to that plane. Back to what the fuck we're doing here. The two things are related. Listen up now, learn yourself something. We'll wrap up this year's harvest in what, two weeks? Three? Then *we'll* be the ones on the planes. Where you figure you'll head for vacation?"

"Hawaii. As usual. Charity and me. Sometimes the north shore waves pick up early, right about when we're done here. I got my best board stored with a buddy at Makaha. A Hawaiian dude. Fuck gins and tonics and tequila sunrises and Irish coffees too. For me on the north shore it'll be nothin' but mai tais and some sweet steep awesome waves. And Charity. She boogie boards the shore breaks. She loves it same as I do."

Shrimp ground his Pall Mall out on the smooth face of the boulder at his side and flipped the squashed butt ten feet into a clump of deer brush. "Well you just answered your own question, dude. We're out here right now so we can keep doin' what we want. That's all there is to it. Where the hell else could you find a job that got you to Hawaii? That gave you the free time? So where the hell else could you be right now? For me it'll be Baja. As usual. You should try it sometime. Maybe there's no surfing, at least not on the Sea of Cortez side, but there's sure as hell sweet fishing and lots else. I'm talking saltwater fly-fishing. Dorado. Roosterfish. Sierra. Bonito, dog snapper, needlefish, skipjack, cabrilla. I can't even *remember* all the species of fish we hook down there. I landed a goddamn sailfish once. That son of a bitch was bigger than me. Took me four hours but I did it. I got that house I rent right on the beach outside Loreto. My boat's right there too, just waitin' for me, with an almost brand-new sixty-horsepower Merc engine. Pretty soon I'll be sittin' out there on the patio at night after a hard day fishing. I'll be buck naked in that warm air sipping some premium tequila. Watching the lightning storms across the sea in mainland Mexico. Sometimes I got a sweet senorita buck naked right there beside me. *Doe* naked I guess it would be. But it ain't just the fishing and the senoritas. I mean, that sea is flat-out beautiful. The water smooth as glass, the offshore islands, the manta rays and flying fish, whales—*blue* whales, *huge* motherfuckers—and dolphin schools swimming along right beside the boat, right in the wake."

"Sounds cool," Shadow said. "Sounds awesome. While you're at it down there, after you get back from fishing I mean, cook yourself up a big pot of brains, lungs, and stomach. Oh yeah, toss in some intestines too. And a couple tongues. Don't forget the balls, either. Then sprinkle it with eyeballs and you and your senorita can dig right in!"

Shadow and Shrimp sat contentedly in sunlight and silence for a while.

The mourning doves called intermittently.

"When we both get back we'll figure it all out about our place, our restaurant. We're out here now because it's the only way we could make us enough money to do what the fuck we want while we're still young. Right?"

"Right," Shadow agreed. "Hell, man, the main reason we argue is so we can pass some time."

"Right," Shrimp said.

"The *only* reason."

"You got it."

Shrimp leaned back into the rock and tilted back his head and closed his eyes. He wished he could take Rainbow with him to Baja. She was the one he wanted naked on the patio at night with the two of them sipping tequila and watching the lightning strikes in the black sky a hundred miles away. He might even have been willing to give up the naked part and take Uncle Sam along too if it was possible. Now he finished his stout and placed the empty bottle back in the Kelty and fished another Pall Mall from his cigarette pack and popped a kitchen match with his thumbnail. He lit up and inhaled deeply. "Hawaii," he said. "Hawaii and Baja. No matter what we eat those're two damn good reasons why the fuck we're here."

"I guess I hear you," Shadow answered. "I mean, I *know* I do."

Shrimp reached into his pants pocket and fingered the good luck stone he always carried with him. The stone was smooth and black and almost perfectly round and close to the size and thickness of a silver dollar. He had found it many years ago on a lonely beach on Carmen Island off Loreto. He knew he didn't truly believe that the stone or anything else could bring him luck but whenever he touched the stone he told himself he believed it.

"We got it pretty much made," Shadow said.

Two rifle shots in quick succession sounded from somewhere far away and echoed off the mountainsides across the valley.

"You hear that?" Shadow said.

"Hear what?"

"Dude, your hearing sucks. Two shots. Sounded like they maybe came from that draw out there by Devil's Horn. Could be a deer hunter."

"No way," Shrimp said.

"That draw's got some humongous fucking bucks."

"Bullshit," Shrimp said. "Too late in the day for a hunter. I'd say we got to be on our fucking toes. I'd say we better watch our asses."

* * *

The retired colonel was high in his new profession's chain of command and felt sure he would steadily work his way to the top. He wore his gray hair cropped close and sported a thin mustache. He was slim and handsome and his old-style olive drab army fatigues had been tailor-made in a shop on Grant Avenue in Chinatown in San Francisco. Miniature binoculars on a narrow black leather strap hung from his neck.

The stocky young man with the homely face standing beside the colonel wore faded jeans and a plaid Pendleton shirt. He had served in the army as a sergeant first class and had been awarded a purple heart and a bronze star. In the months since his discharge his dark blond hair had grown to shoulder-length and he wore his beard neatly trimmed. He was twenty-seven years old and unmarried with no criminal record and had come to the colonel highly recommended by a contact in Missoula.

Recruiting useful employees was a favorite part of the colonel's job and he was here today both to gauge the former sergeant's potential and give him a firsthand look at what could happen in the field.

"So, Robin," the colonel said, "coming from Montana, you're familiar enough with this kind of country."

"I guess," Robin answered. "I worked a lot of years guiding deer and elk hunters in fall and trout fishermen in summer. I liked the hunting best. Not much money in it though. This was way up north in the Yaak Valley. That's some serious country, Colonel."

"Indeed it is. This country right here's no picnic either, and we got up here pretty damn quick. What do you do to stay fit?"

"Run and lift."

"Sounds good."

"Who *is* this Crazy Carlos?" Robin asked the colonel.

"He grows his product a mountain range or two from here. Sells it damn near everywhere. It's a big operation. Not huge like us but big enough. Today he works for us. He's here already. That means we have to be sure our boys don't tangle with one of his boys by mistake."

"Well where is he? Where's his boys?"

"They're here as reserves is all. They're spread around, all over. We won't need them. We need them to think we need them, for now. We need them to think we're on their side is the thing. They're all wearing red headbands and red bandannas. So it's easy. We won't hurt anybody wearing the red."

"I heard this Carlos is a nut job. I heard talk about him in Montana."

"Who in Montana told you that?"

"Dingo."

"Well Dingo might be a nut job himself and Crazy Carlos is a badass for sure, and maybe a nut job along with it. He still packs his army weapon everywhere he goes. Complete with tally notches. Definite kills on one side and possibles on the other. I've been told the stock's almost full. How's that grab you?"

"I think he's a nut job for sure."

"I think you're right. But today, so far as we know, or he knows, he's on our side. Today we deal with the old lady's men. We'll get the old lady's product but we'll leave her and the fat cop alone, for now. We'll deal with the cop sooner or later. Then next year or the year after it'll be Carlos's turn. We'll run him out eventually. Our battles are incremental. One patient step at a time. Do you think of yourself as a patient man?"

"I do. For sure. I found most of my patience tracking elk and finding fish. Mind if I ask you something?"

"I want to find out about you, you want to find out about me. Ask."

"What did you do in the army?"

"I was a battalion commander. And I knew the war was insane from the start. From well before the start. But crazy or not, as a field grade officer I had some opportunities and took advantage of them. Remember when they sent money in, cash money I mean, by the planeload? Billions. It got stolen by practically everybody who could touch it. I took what I figured my share should be, carried it out in my duffle bag, one hundred pounds of one-hundred-dollar bills. A million bucks in hundreds weighs just over twenty-two pounds. Figure it out. That bonus eventually got both of us right here where we are today. Got us started. Look at it this way: a few hundred thousand innocent people died and now millions can torch up their doobs anytime they want in the good old USA. I'm flyin' pretty high right now myself, which is why I'm talking too much. The war was shit from the start and this is where the hundred pounds of hundreds got us both. Tell me what you think about what I just said. What I just told you."

"I think I'm lucky, lucky to be here. I like money too, Colonel. Believe me I do."

"And don't mind what you need to do to get it?"

"Hell no!"

"Good. Now listen up. That old lady—Sunbeam they call her, don't ask me why—she and that fat cop don't know shit. We have the money, we buy people, we buy the information we need. *More* than we need. More people and more information both. Anyway, I learned Sunbeam has a son who went to a high-class college back east and makes plenty of money at a respectable job. So if she's smart maybe she'll move in with him wherever he is and retire. Babysit her grandchildren. The fat cop? Right now I can't even remember his name. I think it's a season of the year. Summer, or Winter. Or a day. Friday, Sunday. Anyway, the crucial thing is they don't have any idea who we are and they got even less of an idea what's actually happening. That's the key thing—we keep anybody we go up against ignorant of what's actually going on!"

"I understand that. I get it. Sure."

"There's also a local yokel they call the Big Dude who's supposed to help Sunbeam and her cohort. But they don't amount to much. None of these people amount to anything, really. But we still plan carefully for everything. You can't really plan ahead in a genuine war, but you can in this, so we do it."

"What happens when somebody tries to double-cross us?"

"Good question. Sooner or later damn near everybody in this business double-crosses everybody else, or tries to. But we're top dogs for now. And the reason we're top dogs is we always know exactly what's happening, because we plan carefully, and because we plan ahead. We know what's happening, but nobody else does. That's the key. Another key is, we hire good men. How many combat tours did you do?"

"Four. Two in each shit hole."

"Exactly how long have you been out?"

"Exactly six months and three days. Wait a minute. Make it four days."

"It'll take you a while to get settled into a new life of serious and complicated commerce. It takes more than six months. I think you can work your way up here, but it takes two or three years to get over a war, if you're lucky. I had the bad nightmares for nearly three years."

"I got the nightmares too."

"How bad?"

"Bad enough. One fucked up one especially. Want to hear it?"

"Sure. We have time. Shoot."

"It's I'm walking down some road. In full gear. It's so hot I'm melting. All my dead buddies are walking up ahead of me down the same road so I figure out it's the road to fucking death that I'm on. And I'm on it. They're up ahead and they're already dead so I know I will be soon too. I'll be next. You can hear explosions up ahead but it's too smoky to see what's happening. You can hear screaming after the explosions. It's so smoky I can't see more than thirty, forty yards. All I can see is about two dozen guys I knew, dead guys, walking along. So I yell at them to stop and turn around 'cause they're going to get it up ahead but they never turn around. They can't hear me. And I don't turn around either. I can't. There's crowds of guys behind me forcing me along, the way it is on a crowded street. Next thing is I start seeing body parts alongside the road. Hands, feet, arms, legs, heads, even bloody balls and dicks. Then all of a sudden there's a huge explosion and I'm in it. It's loud and bright and hot and hurts like crazy and then I'm gone, I'm dead I guess it has to be, and that's when I wake up and sometimes I'm screaming. I don't have it too often. Every two, three weeks. Sometimes I go a month. It sucks no matter how long it is though. Fucking sucks."

"But you're dealing with it."

"Oh yeah, I'm dealing with it."

"That's the main thing, Robin. All I can do that might help is quote a Norman Mailer character from his Second World War novel *The Naked and the Dead*: 'Fugg the goddamn mother-fugging army.' I'm a retired light colonel talking and the Mailer character got it just about right. He summed my sentiments up just about perfectly. 'Fugg' by the way was the word Mailer's editors insisted he use back in the day, before everybody up to and possibly including nuns started saying 'fuck' all the time."

"Do you still have nightmares? I mean, if you don't mind me asking."

"Why would I mind telling you my worst dream? It's interesting, a different variety, not really a nightmare. It comes every few months and I never know when to expect it. In mine I have to move to Detroit, an American city I know well and loathe. After I arrive in town realtors show me houses up for sale but every place I look at is more of a dump than the last one I looked at. Day after day it goes on that way. Then one morning when it's pouring rain I'm supposed to meet a new realtor in a supermarket parking lot. I get there early, so I go inside to shop and when I'm halfway back to my car a jar of blue cheese salad dressing falls out of my shopping cart but it doesn't break. It rolls away. So I chase it, but it keeps rolling away under cars, pickups, vans, and I have to dodge other people pushing their shopping carts while I chase. But I can't catch up with the salad dressing, in fact I'm losing ground steadily, and the realization occurs to me that I'm going to have to spend the rest of my life chasing a jar of blue cheese salad dressing through an endless parking lot in Detroit in the rain. That's my recurring nightmare, Robin. And I'll admit that it scares the living shit out of me. I don't even like blue cheese."

"Wow. No offense, but that's definitely weird."

"I grant you it is, son. But now it's time for us to drop the nightmares and dreams and for you to listen up. See that lone tall pine tree skylighted straight across over there?" The colonel pointed. "Take the binocs here in a minute. Start at the tree and go left to that rock outcropping. Right above the rocks there's a bunch of scrub oaks. On the right side of the oaks two men showed up. Must be Sunbeam's boys. One took his shirt off. Talk about tattoos. Right now those two're lounging around like they're on a company picnic. Alert? They're barely awake. When something serious is at stake there's nothing worse than carelessness, Robin, as I'm sure you know." The colonel cleared his throat with the sound of a dog growling and then spat a mouthful of phlegm onto the earth and handed the binoculars to Robin.

CRAZY CARLOS

These were widely circulated rumors concerning the life lived by the man known as Crazy Carlos:

It took him only three years to graduate from an Ivy League university with a BA in philosophy and a 4.0 grade point average.

He worked his way through school by dealing weed to undergraduates.

Among his fellow philosophers his favorite thinkers were Schopenhauer and Kierkegaard and Spinoza but it had been the novelists Dostoyevsky and Camus and Kafka who most influenced his life. He reread Dostoyevsky's Crime and Punishment *and Camus's* The Stranger *and Kafka's* The Metamorphosis *at least three times each year and he believed with unqualified certainty that these writers had been correct. There was no god and life was absurd and none of us were anything more or less than overgrown insects.*

A professor he seduced told a porn producer she knew about his oversized penis and this led to a short career in adult films.

Because porn didn't pay enough he returned to drugs.

Through the first six years of his drug career he had personally disposed of rivals by either strangulation or gunshot. Whenever practical he forced his victims to choose between a short length of clothesline or a snub-nosed .32.

When drunk or stoned he often bragged about having become the most enormous insect of them all.

He has pictures of children he's fathered tattooed on his arms. Some say there are six boys and five girls and others say six girls and five boys.

TICKS IN THE SPRING

"I can't believe I was scheduled to get tattooed today," Toon said.

"Hey," Shakespeare answered. "Somebody's right over there across from us. Right across there directly underneath that big ol' white cloud that looks kind of like a set of tits, right near that snag."

"Bullshit."

"I shit you not. I saw the fucking reflection off their binoculars. Had to be binoculars."

"You got binoculars to look back?"

"No."

"Why the fuck not?"

"You got binoculars?"

"No."

"Why the fuck not?"

"Cause I figured you did."

"Well I figured you did."

"Well then we're semi-fucked."

"Maybe it's Crazy Carlos's dudes. Probably is. Or could even be Crazy Carlos himself."

"Or the fucking FBI."

"Or the CIA."

"Or the Supreme Court."

"Or the ATF."

"What's the ATF?"

"Alcohol, Tobacco and Firearms."

"Well then, you got your trusty firearm handy?"

"Got my Kalashnikov. My alcohol and tobacco too."

They had stopped above a granite outcropping at a small and comfortable clearing where lush green grass grew on almost level ground. Toon dropped both his fatigue shirt and T-shirt onto the grass between his weapon and his pack. He stretched his arms over his head and lowered them and then casually inspected the tattoo he could best observe. Squinting down at his own chest Elmer Fudd's double-barreled shotgun appeared to be aiming right between his eyes. "I mean, I was scheduled to get my *ass* tattooed today," he said.

"Don't leave your shirts in the grass like that," Shakespeare said. "There's ticks all over the place around here. They'll get inside your shirt and suck your blood, man. They'll suck you dry. You'll maybe even pick up lyme disease."

"When there's ticks all over the place is in the spring," Toon said. "Mostly in March. April too but not as bad as March. Buy yourself a calendar. This right now is early fall."

"Well there's fucking ticks in fall too. Where do you figure they go to in the fall? Hawaii? Cabo San Lucas?"

"Bullshit. There's no ticks in the fall. Hardly any anyway."

"Bullshit."

"You see any more reflections across over there, any binoculars?"

"Nope."

"Well maybe what you saw was some ticks with their shades on heading for Waikiki. Maybe they already boarded their plane. Or I guess they'd fly over on a goose or a heron or a seagull. All I know for sure is, I wish I was getting Dagwood and Mr. Dithers tattooed on my ass right now instead of sitting around out here worrying about weed."

"Well I got my serious issues too. My problems."

"Supercock, right?"

"Hell yes Supercock. I been working *hard* on that novel. I been working my ass off for *years!*"

"So you want to get your great novel you been working your ass off for years on published."

"Fuckin' A I do. Why wouldn't I? But I don't want to be a commercial *sell*out. I never said it's a completely great novel. But it's *good*. Or it'll be good when I get finished. *Damn* good."

"Then turn that New York dude you talked to down."

"Then maybe I won't even get it published at all though. Those New York assholes think we're a bunch of fucking hicks out here."

"But even if you don't get it published at least you won't be a fucking sellout. At least you'll have that."

"I got all *kinds* of cool ideas about how Supercock can use his cock to be a hero. As a lasso. I did that scene already, I know I told you about it, the rodeo scene. As a fly line. I mean, hell, he could break every fly-casting record in the book. What the hell, he can paint his cock up all colorful like a giant snake down in the Florida Everglades, or like a rattlesnake in this country out here. I already got some good ideas about that. He can turn it into a totem pole in Indian country. He can use it like a barrier rope to hold back the crowds at the US Open. That matters, 'cause I can put a terrorist with a fucking bomb in the crowd. He can—"

"You mean the US golf open?"

"Shit yes. What other open would it be?"

"I thought maybe tennis."

"There's no ropes to hold back crowds in tennis. The people sit in bleachers. He could—"

"Use your fuckin' head for a change. You know where the US tennis open is? New York. Where's the editor dude you talked to from? New York! Okay, have it your way, forget the rope. Why couldn't you turn his cock into the net on a tennis court? Then the net could snag the guy with the bomb. Maybe if you put in enough New York scenes they'll forget you're a hick from out west."

"That might work. The tennis thing as a scene I mean. I give you credit. But I know totally for sure Supercock could tie a hangman's noose on his cock and use it in an execution in someplace like Utah. An innocent guy gets convicted. And Supercock knows he's innocent. So after the executioner springs open the trapdoor, that little door on the gallows, he'd let the guy, the condemned man, down nice and easy. Then he'd turn him loose. You can only execute a dude once, I read that someplace, so after he got let down he'd be free. He could—"

"They use firing squads in Utah. I know that for sure because I read it in some book once. They execute guys in Utah with rifles. Or maybe they don't even execute people at all anymore in Utah. Shit yeah, I bet they don't. The trend is totally against it. All we do now is shoot innocent people in wars. Drop bombs too. And fire missiles. But if you put in an execution scene at least make it a New York execution. See what I'm tryin' to tell you?"

"What prison's in New York?"

"Sing Sing I think."

"Okay, Sing Sing it is then. But he could use his cock in so many cool ways! He could turn it into an anchor chain on a yacht. Even on an ocean liner. Or he could stretch it across the field and make it the fifty-yard line at the Super Bowl. Or better yet he could make it that yellow line across the field they mark first down yardage with. The ideas keep bouncing into my head but all the New York dude wants is stupid fuck scenes. Supercock's a fucking *hero*! A *new* hero! Superman, Captain Marvel, Batman, who needs those boring motherfuckers? Hear what *I'm* sayin'? A *new* hero! That's what we need!"

Shakespeare closed his eyes and clenched his fists and stretched both arms toward the blue sky. After he dropped his arms to his sides and opened his eyes the two of them began pacing around their clearing in opposite directions with Shakespeare going clockwise. "You think I'm whacked out?" he asked.

"No," Toon answered. "Why would I, man? More people figure I'm whacked out than figure you are."

"Yeah, well, you're the only totally normal dude I know. We *need* fucking heroes though, we need a new hero, even if he's only in a made-up story. I won't even describe the parody thing I got going along with everything else in the story. It's a book that works on different levels, know what I mean?"

"I guess so. Yeah. I get it."

"I mean, you know the real reason why I write? I *got* to write. The reason I got to is, it's the only way I can try to figure out the way this fucked up world *should* be." Shakespeare glimpsed a moving flash of something small and bright within a willow thicket across the valley alongside a tributary creek. He didn't comment on it. "If I kind of get it straightened out in my head and write it down I can keep *myself* straight at least. Maybe I can even help keep other people straight too. That's all. That's all I want. See what I'm saying?"

"Yeah, well, my tattoos keep me straight. You understand what they mean?"

"That the world's a slaughterhouse. You told me that about six hundred times. Six *thousand*."

"What I'm saying is, we both see most stuff the exact same way. Neither one of us is whacked out. The fucking world's whacked out way more than we are."

"Take a look at all that weed down there in the sun. All that prime cannabis. You ever feel guilty about what we do?"

Toon stopped walking and laughed out loud. He stood shading his eyes with one hand looking down at the ripe product growing as profusely as the corn on any farm in Iowa. "Guilty?" he said. "Are you serious? The way I see it is we're doing the world a huge favor. You think people'd be better off with meth? Booze? Crack? Smack? Coke? Moon gas? Angel dust? Fuck no! I'm totally good with what we do. My advice to you is, you better start dreaming up some fuck scenes for your Supercock hero. You get those scenes good enough, then you can talk the New York asshole into letting him be a hero too. A parody. And whatever else you got in mind. A hero or a parody that does some fucking, that's all. Sounds totally natural to me. If he has a super cock why shouldn't he use it like we all do?"

"Another thing I wonder about is, how come we can't get together and *talk* to these outsider assholes trying to move in on us? How come there's not room for all of us to do business? There *is* room. Look at all this open country, man. There *is* enough money for everybody. There can be. There *should* be. This shit is turning crazy."

"Enough's not enough for most people, that's why. You know that. This is the twenty-first century, man. This is America, the greatest fucking country on earth. Nobody wants enough anymore. They want *more* than enough, everything they can fucking *get*! Forget that shit and figure ways for Supercock to fuck and be a hero and a parody too."

"Maybe you're right."

"Maybe?"

"Okay, dude, yeah, you are."

* * *

"Care for some dried peaches, Robin?" asked the colonel.

"Yes please."

"I'm something of a health nut. All dried fruit's good. Peaches are best though."

"Thanks."

"Like to hear an informative anecdote to go along with the health food?"

"I would. Sure."

"First, I want you to appreciate the fact that when you work for us you always need to be thorough at your job. What we ask might seem extreme at first, but it isn't. So, when Crazy Carlos entered the equation I set out to learn everything I could about him. He actually has a Facebook page. And he definitely lives up to his name. I learned that he's starting up a company in a small town someplace east of here. Apparently he plans to go into the ammunition business. Not just selling ammo but manufacturing it. His bullets are going to be laced with pork. He'll market them wherever people hate Muslims because, get this, if you shoot and kill a Muslim with a pork-laced bullet he'll miss out on his crowd of virgins and travel straight to hell. According to Crazy Carlos that is. I can't wait to see his advertising campaign. Porky Pig should be his spokesman. The point, finally, is that this is exactly the kind of knowledge we might be able to use to do him in when the time comes. We never know beforehand exactly what we can use, but the more we know the better off we are. It's never possible to know too much."

"Why'd you get in this business, Colonel?"

"I'd rather make people happy than kill them. That's about it. You'll learn to appreciate what we do. The two things to remember, the most important things always, are to prepare adequately, *more* than adequately, and to do whatever you're required to do aggressively. And remember that no detail is too small to be handled properly and carefully. One small example: last night, midnight it was, I arranged to use a man stuffing his fat face with buffalo burgers to my distinct advantage. To our advantage I should say."

"How'd you do that, Colonel? Why'd you do it?"

"It was a single minor detail in a big, complicated picture. Here's the bottom line though: We specialize in intimidation. Sometimes death becomes a necessary sideline. Death sends messages. More peaches?"

* * *

Canada geese traveling south passed over the valley in long skeins and perfectly formed Vs and at such high altitudes that few on the ground saw them and no one heard their honking.

More than an hour passed as the geese flew and dozens of men in pairs and larger groups remained concealed in the wooded hills overlooking acres of marijuana worth tens of millions of dollars. They sat and talked or stood and talked or paced and talked and waited for something to happen. They smoked tobacco and weed and ate sandwiches and drank beer and ale and tequila. They all knew that sooner or later something would happen but only the colonel knew exactly what and when it would be.

Shakespeare and Toon had found a fallen Douglas fir with a smooth gray weathered trunk that lay at just the right height for their backs as they sat with outstretched legs on the hard ground. Nearby on the low limb of a healthy fir two crows sat perched close together airing their wings and loosing loud caws that echoed faintly from across the valley.

"Those two dudes, those crows I mean, remind me of somebody," Toon said.

"Heckle and Jeckle," Shakespeare answered.

"How the hell'd you know that?"

"A wild guess. But I'm not as dumb as I look."

"I hope you're not, dude."

"You're the dumb one, man."

"Says who?"

"Says me."

"Why?"

"'Cause you almost went and got Dagwood Bumstead, a geek, and Mr. Dithers, an asshole businessman, tattooed on your ass."

"Who says that's dumb?"

"I do."

"Oh yeah? Well why?"

"You been in the army, right? The greatest army in the world, right? The greatest army in history. The fucking politicians say it all the time."

"So?"

"So this. I been thinking it over. It's so fucking obvious. There's a cartoon about soldiers, right? A cartoon with two soldiers in it, two enlisted men, and these two would make a fucking lot better tattoo than a geek and an asshole businessman. I mean, there's more than two soldiers in the cartoon, but two main ones."

"What cartoon? What fucking enlisted men?"

"Think about it, okay? Use your brain for a change."

"What cartoon?"

"You're the goddamn cartoon scholar. If they taught cartoons in colleges you'd be a PhD, a professor. Hell, man, you'd be president of Cartoon College. *Think* about it."

"No need to scream, man. Look at that, you went and spooked Heckle and Jeckle away."

They heard the two crows caw loudly and watched them flap their way up over the trees and fly off side by side high across the valley.

"Beetle Fucking Bailey," Shakespeare said.

"Holy shit!" Toon said, striking his forehead with the heel of his hand. "You're *right*!"

"Fucking A I'm right. Beetle Bailey and Sergeant Snorkel. I mean, dude, Snorkel's after Beetle every fucking *week*! Snorkel's been beating the shit out of Beetle Bailey for a hundred years! Fifty at least. Today saved you, man. If you'd got the Dagwood-Dithers tatt it'd've been too late! Now you got a clean slate, a bare white ass ready for some good shit! Right?"

Toon's thin lips formed a sheepish smile and he shook his head and then struck his forehead again. "Thanks, man," he said. "I mean, I definitely *owe* you one! What it proves is, it's true what they say. The shit right in front of your eyes, that's the shit you don't see!"

* * *

Shadow and Shrimp sat leaning against opposite sides of the round gray boulder underneath the sugar pine. They were watching and listening but since the distant rifle shots they hadn't heard or seen anything unusual.

"Maybe it *was* a hunter," Shadow said.

"Maybe not," Shrimp answered. He emptied his stout and tossed the empty bottle as far as he could and after a few seconds they heard it shatter against rock.

"I got to drain the dragon," Shrimp said. He stood and looked out at the country and then stretched and unzipped his fly and walked ten paces and stepped around the trunk of the sugar pine.

"You'll kill that damn tree pissing on it," Shadow said.

"I'll nourish it you mean."

Shrimp zipped up and came back and sat in the shade a few feet from Shadow.

"What the hell, I better piss too," Shadow said.

He got up and walked to the sugar pine and pissed and zipped up and walked back. "I got a fucking stone in my boot," he said. "How'd that happen?"

Shadow sat and unlaced his right boot and pulled it off and emptied out the stone.

Shrimp saw that two bright white clouds had formed directly over the valley floor. The largest had the shape of a fish with its big mouth wide open and to Shrimp it appeared to be closing in on the smaller cloud that reminded him of a baitfish trying to escape a predator. He wondered why exactly the same things had to happen everywhere. Humans hunted down other humans to kill them and the clouds chased other clouds across the sky. "All I know for sure is it's a crazy fucking world," he said.

"Listen," Shadow said.

"What?"

Shadow pointed north. "Just shut the fuck up and listen!"

"What'd you hear?"

Shadow pointed again and whispered: "Listen!"

Both Shrimp's eardrums had been ruptured but now when he turned his head and cupped his left hand around his left ear and concentrated he thought he could hear distant footfalls moving through the forest.

Shadow was pulling his boot back on and now there were more footfalls and they were easier to hear because they were closer.

"Sit still!" a deep voice said. "Freeze, motherfuckers!"

Shrimp was running. He looked back over his shoulder once and saw Shadow running ten yards behind him and he heard the weapon open up and saw Shadow's chest explode in gouts of blood.

Shadow had vanished and Shrimp kept sprinting with his head down and his arms and legs pumping as hard as he could make them go and he swerved through trees with rounds whining and buzzing by and several rounds smashed into a tree close beside him spraying bark, and another round whined off a rock on the same side and then there were voices screaming.

He was sick and dizzy and had no idea what the voices said and after a few more seconds the voices were gone and then the firing stopped too and Shrimp kept running and dodging between trees and he heard his feet pounding and realized he was sprinting down a steep hill.

At the bottom of the hill he came to a small creek lined with buck brush and willow thickets and occasional clumps of poison oak and he crashed through the buck brush and jumped the creek and labored up the hill on the other side.

Oak trees grew on this north-facing slope and there were band-tailed pigeons feeding on the fallen acorns under the trees. As he passed close to the big birds they flapped into noisy flight with the tips of their wings clapping together underneath them as they lifted off the ground.

Shrimp recovered his senses.

He knew he wasn't being chased and now he knew exactly where he was. This was the narrow draw where a year ago, or it might have been two, he had been searching for Indian artifacts and had treed a bobcat. The startled male cat had been feeding on a jackrabbit and Shrimp remembered how the cat had leaped onto an oak limb and under his weight the long limb had dropped so low that Shrimp could have reached and touched the cat if he'd been dumb enough to want to.

He remembered that the small creek behind him led between steep slopes all the way to Samson Creek, which was a major tributary through the valley.

He was certain that at least for now no one was after him and he turned and jogged back down the hill through the oaks. He was sweating hard and panting for breath and his thighs burned. A few more pigeons took flight and others perched motionless on oak limbs near the tops of trees and watched him with beady black eyes.

Shrimp identified the bobcat tree and stopped to look at the limb where the treed cat had crouched on its long legs with his back arched staring at him.

"Hello, buddy," Shrimp remembered telling the cat as he walked up.

The big cat had stared at him with bright green eyes and long gray whiskers and a lustrous coat and short black pointed tufts on his ears.

Shrimp and the cat had stared at each other eye to eye with the cat less than an arm's length away.

"You sure don't look scared," Shrimp said. "What would you do if I scratched between your ears, dude?"

The bobcat never moved and never blinked and breathed slowly.

"What about it?" Shrimp said. "Would you rip my damn arm at least half off?"

The bobcat's left ear twitched.

"I figure that means yes."

Shrimp had looked into the cat's eyes for a minute or more and then turned and started up the draw. Searching along both banks of the creek that afternoon he found a handful of obsidian chips and three perfect bird points in less than an hour. When he hiked back downstream the bobcat was gone along with the jackrabbit.

Now far behind him he heard gunfire. He knelt and drank from the creek. The water ran pure and sweet and cold with nothing anywhere upstream to foul it. He cupped cold water onto his face and over the top of his head and then began jogging downstream along the north bank toward the reservoir. He stayed close beside the creek except when he circumvented willow thickets.

He thought about Shadow.

A covey of mountain quail flushed with loudly whirring wings from a dense thicket. The big birds scattered in all directions and before the last quail had disappeared into cover a black-tailed doe crashed out of the next thicket down and bounded up the hill and quickly disappeared among the oaks.

By the time he had gone about a mile Shrimp was sweating hard again.

Then he saw an unarmed bare-chested man with his head down sprinting upstream toward him through the brush and he veered into the next thicket he reached and planted his feet solidly with his weapon ready.

He watched the man continue toward him looking down at the ground all the while with his arms flailing as he ran. Then from a distance of thirty or forty yards he could make out Elmer Fudd and Bugs Bunny on the pale bare sweaty chest and he knew it was Toon.

Shrimp forced his way through the supple willow branches and stepped out of the thicket and raised a hand and called out, "Toon!"

Toon stopped short and looked up and then crouched and used a hand to shield his eyes from sunlight. "Shrimp? Is it you?"

"Yeah, man!"

"No shit? Is it you?"

Shrimp stood where he was and Toon ran up and stopped in front of him. "All shit broke loose down below!" he said.

"What shit?"

"They killed Shakespeare!"

"What the fuck? Who did?"

"I got no fucking idea who but they did! I never even saw the motherfuckers and they opened up on us, whoever they were, and I took off running, I never even had a chance to grab my weapon, and they didn't even shoot at me, they yelled at me.

They said, 'Tell everybody what you saw, asshole! *Every*body! Tell
'em what happened here, asshole!' That's what they yelled."

"So they're not coming after you?"

"I never even *saw* the motherfuckers. Never even heard 'em
till they opened up and blew Shakespeare away. That's all I know.
Don't go down there, man. Where's Shadow?"

"Wasted."

"Dead?"

"Yeah, dead."

"What the fuck's going on?"

"I got no idea."

"Well don't go down where I just came from, man!"

"I'm not goin' back where I came from either. But the fuckers
that killed Shadow hardly even chased me."

"Shadow's really dead?"

"Yeah. Really."

"What the fuck should we do?"

"I know this country." Shrimp pointed uphill to his left
through the oak trees. "Straight up there and halfway down the
other side there's an old gold mine. C'mon, man! It's as good a
place as any."

Toon followed Shrimp straight up the hill through the trees.
All the way up he watched Shrimp's boots a few feet ahead of him.
The boots clumped into the soft forest floor of moldered leaves
and acorns and he heard Shrimp breathing hard and he heard his
own deep breathing. He felt his heart pounding in his chest. He
thought he could hear it. Every minute or two he looked back
and once just before they reached the summit he thought he saw

movement through the trees far below them. Then he stumbled and fell to his hands and knees, and then he looked again and saw nothing.

When they finally crested the mountain and started down the other side they found themselves in burned over forest. The oaks were leafless and charred black and many limbless pines had fallen and lay across the ground at odd angles. Bright green grass and darker green brush had grown through the scorched earth. The old mine was almost halfway down the mountainside and Toon followed Shrimp past a small pile of rotted timbers into the dark shaft. When Shrimp stopped abruptly at a point where there was barely light enough to see Toon ran into him from behind.

"Take it easy, man," Shrimp said.

"Sorry."

"This country burned in the Muffin Fire."

"Two summers ago?"

"Two falls ago."

"What if somebody saw us come in here?"

"Nobody saw us."

"What if they did?"

Both men panted for breath and their faces were filmed with sweat. Shrimp stood bent at the waist with his hands on his knees. "Nobody saw us," he said.

"How long you figure we should stay here?"

"Till dark."

"We left fucking footprints all over the place out there."

"Nobody saw us, dude."

"What'll we do when it's dark?"

"Head back. What else?"

"Back where?"

"The Bird of Prey."

"Shit, that must be fifteen miles."

"More like twenty."

Inside the mine shaft it was damp and cool. The air smelled dank and the floor was solidly packed earth and the walls and ceiling were solid rock. Shrimp knew that farther back out of sight in the darkness clusters of bats hung from the ceiling. He sat and leaned back with his arms clasped around his knees. "This sucks but we're okay for now," he said. "You and me've been in serious shit before. How many guys have we seen get wasted? How many buddies? Plenty. Seems like it never fucking ends. It always sucks. For now at least you and me are okay."

"Yeah it sucks," Toon said. "This place does."

"Hey, man. The place reminds me of a song."

"A song?"

"Yeah."

"What song?"

"Old country song. 'She Got the Goldmine (I Got the Shaft).' Remember that one?"

"Yeah I do."

"Well this time we got the fucking shaft."

"We sure as fuck did," Toon said.

The shaft was at least eight feet wide and Toon sat and leaned back against the cold stone wall directly across from Shrimp. He raised his head and closed his eyes against the sweat and then opened his eyes and blinked and looked toward the bright entrance off to his right. "What was that?" he said.

"What was what?" Shrimp answered.

"Didn't you hear it?"

"No."

"You didn't hear anything?"

"No."

"Well I did."

"What?"

"A click," Toon said. "Or more sort of like two stones hitting together."

"I didn't hear it."

"You sure?"

"Hell yes I am."

"Well maybe I got better ears."

"Maybe you don't."

"Shakespeare always figured he'd die in the war," Toon said, "the real war, the one we were in I mean."

"Well it wasn't a real war so maybe that's why he didn't die in it."

Somewhere from the bright sky outside a hawk screamed.

"You hear that?" Toon said.

"Yeah I did. Sure. I guess my ears are okay, right?"

"Maybe."

Somewhere far back in the mine shaft water dripped steadily and slowly.

Outside the hawk screamed again.

"You believe in any kind of god or anything?" Toon asked.

"Hell no," Shrimp answered.

"Me either. But shit, there must be *some* damn thing that makes shit happen."

"There's some kind of power," Shrimp said. "Some kind of force or whatever you want to call it that makes stuff happen. Makes *everything* happen. Nobody knows what it is though. Nobody has any idea. How the hell could anybody know? So they make shit up. Always have, always will."

"You believe in heaven and hell, all that shit?"

"Hell no."

"I'm askin' 'cause of Shakespeare," Toon said. "He figured he should've died in the war, he told me all that. Then when he didn't die in the war he figured he'd get it violently some other way. And he did. You don't figure something made it happen?"

"Hell yes something made it happen. A fucking bullet made it happen. A bunch of bullets did. A whole shitload of bullets."

"He ever talk to you about when he was a kid?"

"No," Shrimp said. "Not much. He said he had some troubles back then. Who the fuck didn't though? But he never said much."

"He did to me. Talked to me about it I mean. One thing was, he felt guilty about stuff he did when he was young."

"Like what?"

"The weird thing was he felt guilty about stuff that wasn't even really bad."

"Like what though?"

"He told me about this teacher he had, the one who first turned him on to Shakespeare. Some dude named Koch except the guys in class called him Kochsucker. Koch's hero was Thoreau. You know about Thoreau? Henry David Thoreau?"

"Shit yes I do. The dude who lived alone in some little cabin someplace out in the woods."

"Yeah, Shrimp. That's the one. Out by some pond. Well this Koch lived in some primitive little cabin too and the cabin had an outhouse and on Halloween night one year Shakespeare and his buddies lifted the outhouse off the hole where all the shit went and set it a few feet back. Then they hid till Koch walked out of his cabin around midnight, before he went to bed they figured, and he walked straight for the outhouse and fell right into the shit hole instead. It was a really dark night, that's why the trick worked, and Shakespeare felt guilty as hell about it, especially later on after he turned into Shakespeare. He never got over it and he figured he'd get paid back for that dirty trick sooner or later. That shitty trick he played."

"Well did the teacher get hurt? Did he drown in the shit?"

"Hell no, Shrimp. He climbed back out was all and Shakespeare and his buddies ran off through the woods laughing their asses off."

"That's way past weird. That's crazy. How could Shakespeare feel guilty about that? That was a cool, classic trick is all."

"I got no idea why he felt guilty but he did. He even cried when he told me about it and he wasn't even drunk or stoned. I mean, that's how guilty the poor dude felt."

"That's totally crazy," Shrimp said.

"Yeah it is. Yeah it was."

They sat in silence and thought about Shakespeare.

"Listen," Toon said. "You hear that water dripping?"

"Yeah I do."

"You hear anything else?"

"Like what?"

"Like anything. Like a faraway four-wheeler. A Rhino it sounds like."

"Nope. No fucking Rhino."

"Well it's out there," Toon said. "You're fucking deaf. I hear it better now. Also sounds like somebody yelling and screaming like a son of a bitch. Sounds like Stones in fact. You can't hear that?"

"No."

"Well you're fuckin' deaf, man."

"How can I be deaf? I hear that dripping. I hear you loud and clear. Did you fart?"

"Yeah I did."

"Yeah, well I heard that too. Why the fuck would anybody fart in a mine shaft, man?"

"'Cause I *had* to."

"Yeah, well, thanks, dude."

Shrimp leaned his head back against the cold stone behind him and stretched his legs straight out in front of him with his hands resting on his thighs and he closed his eyes and listened to the dripping water.

"Shakespeare told me lots of shit," Toon said. "We got stoned together damn near every night over in the zone. I can tell it now 'cause the dude's dead. His old man was the real nut. He was a bus driver. I mean, I bet he's the one who drove Shakespeare nutty. One time they lived in East Oakland, a shitty neighborhood from everything *I* ever heard. Bad shit on the street. Bad shit on his old man's bus. His old lady was dead already, a drug overdose. Smack. Shakespeare figures she was on it when he was born. Anyway, bad shit on the street and the old man's bus, practically every damn day. Some homeboys raped a girl, a *young* girl I'm saying, right on the bus one day. In the *day*time. An' I mean *young*. About twelve. When Shakespeare's old man tried to break it up they beat the shit out of him. He woke up that night in the hospital. He got better but he had to go on disability after that. Shakespeare was about twelve himself then, the same age as that girl who got raped. Well starting right then when that happened Shakespeare's old man nailed the doors shut, the front and the back door, in the little house they lived in. The shack, that's what Shakespeare called it. He boarded up all the windows too. The old man cut a little hole in the roof and strung a rope out the hole and that's how they got in and out of the house, the shack. They climbed up through that hole in the roof and lowered themselves down to the street on that rope. Somebody always had to stay in the house to pull the rope back up and then toss it back out when whoever was out came back and wanted in. How fucking nutty is that? It wasn't Shakespeare's fault he was nuts, that's all I'm sayin'. All Shakespeare ever kind of liked was school. I guess he felt safe there. Protected I guess. Anyway, a few months after Shakespeare shipped off to war or combat or whatever you call it his old man took off south from East Oakland all the way to Mexico, to Baja. To Todos Santos, a little town on the Pacific there, way down south. An' all he did there was play that Eagles song, that "Hotel California," and drink tequila. After a few days he shot himself in his room at breakfast time. An' that goddamn song was still playing when they went in the room after they heard the shot. I hate the Eagles, man. He never told you that shit ever? None of it?"

Shrimp didn't answer.

"He ever tell you that shit or not, dude?"

No answer.

"Hey, man," Toon said. "Ain't you even talkin' to me anymore?" Then he heard the soft snoring and he leaned forward to peer through the near darkness and saw his friend's head tilted to one side with his mouth half open. "Okay, man," he said, "catch yourself some Zs."

Soon Toon fell asleep himself.

Toon dreamed not for the first time about a Mexican girl he had seen picking pears in an orchard farther north. He had been riding along a bike path that bordered long rows of trees laden with ripe fruit. There were acres and acres of the trees and the girl stood somewhere near the middle rung of a stepladder picking pears with both hands and placing the fruit into a sack held in place in front of her by a canvas strap over her shoulders. She wore faded jeans and a sleeveless cotton blouse. Around her neck was a delicate gold chain with a small golden cross. On the hot afternoon her brown face was filmed with sweat. In the glimpse Toon caught of her as he peddled by, her black hair shined in bright sunlight and her slim strong arms and small hands worked quickly and her facial expression showed intense concentration on her labor. Toon stopped peddling and coasted to a stop and lifted his bike around and pushed it back and stopped again a few feet away from the girl on the ladder. Without doubt she was the loveliest girl he had ever seen in his life anywhere. She didn't look at him and showed no sign she knew he was there.

"Hello," he said. *"Hola."*

"Hola," she answered without looking at him.

"Do you have time to talk? *Hable Inglés?"*

"Trabajo," she said without looking at him. She continued quickly picking and carefully placing the big Bartlett pears into the bulging sack.

"I know what that means," Toon said. "Work."

Her tanned skin was smooth and brown and perfect. Everything about her looked perfect to Toon. He stared at her. He couldn't help himself. She kept working until after two or three minutes all the pears she could reach on that tree were in the sack and then she hopped from the ladder to the ground and lifted the ladder in both hands and carried it to the next tree down the row.

Toon climbed onto his bike and peddled away. *"Adios, senorita,"* he called as he passed her by and she didn't look at him and didn't answer.

He peddled back and forth by the same orchard at different times of day for the next three days and he never saw her again and that had happened seven years ago and ever since Toon had dreamed about the Mexican girl two or three times a month. She was the only girl he had ever dreamed about.

Toon was awakened from his dream by a muted rumbling roar and he felt the stone wall against his back and the packed dirt floor underneath him tremble. When the roar and trembling ceased he heard a steady noise like hail pounding against a roof and when that sound stopped he was wide awake.

He knew his eyes were wide open but everything was absolutely black and then he heard the dripping water again. "What the fuck?" he said and he held his right hand inches in front of his open eyes and couldn't see it.

"You okay?"

It was Shrimp.

"Where the fuck are you?" Toon said. "What the fuck just happened?"

"Explosion. A loud blast right outside. Right up above us."

"What?"

"You were still asleep. Right outside, right up above us."

"What? Where are you, man?"

"Right here." Now Shrimp had his hand on Toon's shoulder and he slid his hand to Toon's bicep and squeezed his arm and took his hand away. "I'm right here, dude. You okay? Don't panic."

"So what the fuck happened?"

"Somebody out there set off dynamite and blew half a mountain down overtop of us. Right down over the way we came in. They knew we were here, man."

"How's anybody know?"

"I got no fucking idea."

"Who the fuck's trying to kill us?"

"If whoever it was wanted to kill us they could've walked right on in here and done the job."

"Then why'd they do it? What can we do?"

"I got no idea why they did it Toon ol' buddy. But I sure as shit know what we can do."

"What?"

"Dig."

"Dig our way out?"

"With our hands."

"It's so fuckin' *dark*."

Toon felt Shrimp's hand back on his arm and this time Shrimp was pulling at him. "This way. We got to start. The air in here sucks but it'll last a while."

"Got any matches?"

"No sense burning up the air. Let's fuckin' dig, dude."

* * *

So Shrimp and Toon dug.

They scooped handfuls of dry earth from the pile that sealed the entrance to the mine shaft and they tossed the earth behind them as far as they could throw it. Soon the heavy moisture-laden air in the shaft grew noticeably warmer. The sweat of the two men increased the humidity around them and caused them to sweat more profusely. The earth they dug was a kind of coarse-grained dust that caked under their fingernails and coated their hands and arms and faces. Both men panted with exertion and their noses and mouths and throats became coated with dry dust. For a while they coughed up phlegm and then the coughs turned dry. Every few minutes with the intervals growing shorter as they worked and as their fatigue grew the two of them made their way through the darkness to the place where warm water dripped from the cave's ceiling onto the floor. They couldn't see the large puddle they stood in while they drank but after several trips the water leaked through their boots and soaked their socks. They stood in the puddle and took turns catching drops of water in their opened mouths.

"It's harder to breathe already," Toon said in a raspy voice as he stood in the hot wet darkness waiting for Shrimp to give him his turn at the dripping water.

"I got to shit," Shrimp said as he stepped away.

"Well go on back there a ways to shit," Toon said as he tilted his head upward and opened his mouth wide. The first drop of water hit his forehead. After he adjusted his stance a drop hit his nose and after another slight adjustment the third drop fell into his mouth. He heard Shrimp shuffling his feet as he moved farther back into the shaft and he counted the drops and swallowed after every ten. After fifty drops he stepped away. "It tastes like shit," he said. "Like fucking sulfur. Did those gold miners use chemicals? Mercury or some shit? Anyway fifty drops is my limit." When he leaned forward to let the drops of water hit the top of his head or the back of his neck a long loud resonating bowel explosion sounded from a few yards away. "Jesus Christ," he said. "You think the poison water did it to you? If you were on a toilet seat that there would've lifted you two feet high. I'm goin' back to dig."

"My bad," Shrimp said.

A minute after Toon began digging Shrimp was back and the two men scooped earth with both hands and tossed it behind them.

"My fuckin' *pants*'re stickin' to me with sweat," Shrimp said after a while.

"Mine too."

"You know what life is?"

"Yeah," answered Toon. "A pain in the ass."

"Worse, man."

"A royal pain in the ass?"

"Way worse. Life's a kick square in the fuckin' balls and a bucket of piss poured over your head."

"That water back there tastes like piss."

"Yeah, and we got to drink it."

"All I know is, soon's I get back to town I'm gettin' Beetle Bailey an' Sergeant Snorkel tattooed on my ass."

"What happened to Dagwood Bumstead?"

"Changed my mind is all," Toon said.

"How come?"

"Dagwood's a dork."

"So's Beetle Bailey."

"Yeah, well at least he's a soldier."

"So that's good?"

"A soldier beats a businessman dork any damn day."

"What the fuck are we doing here in some fucking mine shaft talking about this shit? Beetle fucking Bailey. I mean, I figured there was a fifty-fifty chance—*better* than fifty-fifty— that today would be another regular day, maybe a little ass-kicking at the most. There's *always* rumors, *always* dudes talking about big-time rippers moving in, about tough, super-tough, dudes from someplace else. Well it fucking *happened*. Shadow's *wasted*. Our plans are fucking *fucked*. Our restaurant." Shrimp coughed hard and pounded his fist against his chest until finally the coughing stopped. "So all that fucking leaves is, let's fucking dig," he said.

Though their pace had slowed considerably they kept digging. The air grew warmer and heavier and Toon's eyes burned and Shrimp's throat was so sore that despite his thirst he decided against going back for more rancid water.

"How much dirt you figure's piled here?" Toon asked. "How many fucking tons?"

"A lot. The whole goddamn mountain shook when that charge went off."

"Well how long you figure this'll take?"

"I got no idea. But we got to do it. You want out?"

"Yeah."

"Then dig."

* * *

As they worked in exhausted silence Shrimp remembered a squad patrol a few weeks before he was shipped home. The sergeant's name was Bumgard and Shrimp and the other squad members regarded him as a stupid cracker asshole because all he ever did was look for trouble even if there wasn't any. That day Bumgard had looked hard but they found no trouble anywhere and they finally reached a small hut at the end of a dirt street. Bumgard kicked the door in and they followed him into a small room with a few straw mats on the floor and an old wooden crate for a table with a couple of empty bottles sitting on the crate. The young woman standing beside the crate was one of the prettiest females

Shrimp had ever seen anywhere. Her head was uncovered and she wore a loose-fitting white dress. Her hair was black as a crow's wing and her skin was smooth and her eyes were like fire and she held a baby girl in her arms. The baby girl might have been two years old and it was already plain to see that someday she would look much like her mother. Shrimp was surprised when he realized that the baby wasn't afraid and neither was the mother. The mother stared at Bumgard with the fire in her eyes turned to ice. "Out!" the mother said. "Go!" She knew that much English. She pointed at the rickety door that Bumgard had kicked in. "Back outside, men," Bumgard said in his squeaky cracker voice. "Ain't nothin' for us here." Shrimp was the last one out of the hut and the last thing he did was smile at the lovely mother and wave his free hand at her. When the mother gave him a tiny smile and waved back Shrimp felt good for the first time in more than a year. He remembered the mother and daughter often and hoped they had made it.

"Gotta sit down," Toon said.

"Yeah," Shrimp agreed. "Fuckin' A, man."

They sat in the hot, wet stifling darkness with their aching backs against the high pile of dirt they'd made behind them with their digging.

"I guess I can climb back up in a while," Shrimp said. "In a few minutes. Maybe." When he heard himself speak it sounded like the voice of a stranger. The muscles had cramped in his hands and he found he could no longer bend his fingers. He had periodic dry heaves and every few minutes since shitting his stomach muscles had cramped spasmodically and his calf muscles were cramping too and his wet feet burned inside his boots. When he wiped his face with the back of his hand he realized his skin was coated not with dust but with something more like slimy mud. His throat was so sore he could barely swallow and every time he took a deep breath stabs of pain coursed through both lungs.

"We might die in here," he said.

"You think?"

"You?"

"Yeah," Toon said, "I guess."

"Yeah we might."

"Maybe somebody'll look for us though. Dig us out."

"Who?"

"The guys. Somebody."

"Nobody knows we're here. Nobody gives a shit about an old mine shaft either. Hardly anybody even knows this place is here."

"You want to go back for water?" Toon said.

"No," Shrimp answered.

"I guess I can hack it."

"Hack what?"

"Dying. Croaking. Death."

"If we die we got no choice," Shrimp said. "We got to hack it."

"How many guys you seen die? How many people?"

"Dozens. *Hundreds.*"

"Me too. Hundreds. What the fuck's it all for?"

"Nobody knows," Shrimp said.

"Nobody?"

"*Nobody.*"

"Well, shit, then at least I'm not the only one."

"The only one what?"

"The only one who doesn't know jack shit."

"Nobody knows jack shit about dying."

"Nobody?"

"Nobody," Shrimp repeated. "People pretend is all. Like religious people. Like assholes with education."

"You ready to get back up?"

"Almost."

"I think I got to get some water."

Shrimp sat motionless with his eyes closed and his arms at his sides and his legs outstretched. With every minute that passed it seemed harder to breathe and he felt progressively worse. Now his stomach burned and his head throbbed. When he tried pressing the back of his head into the dirt piled behind him the pain grew worse.

"What the fuck," Toon muttered. "Too fucking much *dirt*. I can't even fucking get *by* here."

"Can't get by where?" Shrimp asked in his croaking voice. His throat felt raw now and the pain grew worse every time he tried to speak or swallow.

"Can't get by this fuckin' *dirt*," Toon answered. "We piled so much up I can't even get *by* anymore. We're cut off from the fuckin' water!"

Shrimp heard Toon scraping at the dirt with both hands. He imagined him digging like a dog that was making a hole to bury a bone and the image in his mind almost made him smile.

He heard Toon stop digging.

"We don't deserve this, man," Toon said.

"You sound like Clint Eastwood, man. In that cowboy movie."

"What?"

"Clint Eastwood."

"Cowboy movie?"

"Yeah."

"Never saw it."

"You saw it with *me,* man."

"Way back?"

"Way back, before the war."

"War? What war?"

"Fuck you."

"What's it about?"

"The movie?"

"Yeah."

Shrimp heard Toon sit back down beside him.

"The movie?" Shrimp said again.

"Yeah."

"Hurts me to fucking talk. It started out with some whore kidding a cowboy about his tiny little dick. In the whorehouse. The one with the tiny dick's in the whorehouse with his friend. So after the whore makes fun of the guy's dick he cuts her up and after that Clint Eastwood and some black dude and some kid come to town to kill the one with the tiny dick and his friend. The whores collected money to pay whoever killed the two cowboys." Shrimp remembered the movie well but it hurt too much to keep talking. "I forget what all happens after that," he said.

"So what's it got to do with what we deserve?"

"Some badass sheriff Clint Eastwood's about to blow away says he doesn't deserve to die. So Clint Eastwood says, 'Deserve's got nothin' to do with it.' That's what he said and I figure he was right. That's the fucking point. My fucking throat's on fire though. I can't hardly talk anymore."

"All we ever wanted to do was make a decent living. That's all we ever wanted to do, man."

Toon sat next to Shrimp. Leaning back against the dirt he could hear Shrimp and judged him to be no more than a couple of feet away. He heard his own raspy breathing. Now it felt as if someone had stuffed a dry rag down his throat.

After every third or fourth breath Toon let out a long sigh. He could smell Shrimp and then he wondered if he might be smelling himself. Then he thought he was smelling them both.

Rapid random thoughts drifted through Toon's mind. He remembered when he and a buddy had cut class in high school to go swimming out at the lake on a sunny day and they needed an excuse afterward so they took bottle caps out of a trash can and cut their own faces up and then went back to school with their faces scraped and cut and bloodied and claimed they'd been attacked and beaten by a town gang at lunchtime, and the lie worked. He remembered a camping trip he'd taken with his dad when he was ten. Eleven. First they'd dug worms and then they'd fished in a river near the campground and Toon caught the biggest trout and his dad had taken a picture and the framed picture with Toon and his monster trout had hung on their living room wall up until Toon left home for the army. Toon had never been back home and he wondered if the picture might still be there in the living room. If it was hanging there still he wondered what else if anything he'd leave behind when he died. If he died in this mine shaft and nobody found him even his tattoos would be gone and even if they did find his dead body they'd put him in a box and bury him somewhere in a hole and the tattoos would be gone six feet under anyway. His parents were poor and the cheapest thing would be to bury him in the nearest military cemetery. He remembered his first steady girlfriend when he was seventeen and how he copped her cherry in the backseat of a car he borrowed and parked out by the golf course and how it was the only cherry he ever copped in his life. He wondered where she was now and he figured no matter where she was or who she was married to she remembered him too because girls must remember the guys who copped their cherries. He remembered when he got motor pool grease on his canteen cover and stole a clean canteen cover to replace his ratty one from a guy he didn't like in another platoon because he needed the clean one to pass Saturday inspection and the platoon sergeant of the guy he stole it from reported Toon to the company commander and then a friend of Toon's who clerked in the supply room lied to the company commander and claimed he'd issued Toon the new canteen cover an hour before inspection, and that lie worked too.

Toon heard Shrimp's labored breathing beside him in the darkness. In the space of a minute the raspy breaths came quickly and then slowed and then quickened again. Then there was a lapse of several seconds when no breath came and then finally Toon heard a drawn-out sigh.

Toon knew he could do no more digging. He felt far too tired and too dizzy and too sick to work. He realized he was too far gone to get up on his feet and he knew for certain he would die here and with that realization another memory came suddenly and clearly to his mind.

Before he went to war he did his basic training down south and then his advanced eight weeks out west and then after that he had been issued orders for Nuremberg where he worked as a mechanic in a motor pool. Before the army he had always been poor and hated being poor and soon after he arrived in Nuremberg Toon fell into a strict routine. He worked hard all month and ate in the mess hall and slept in the barracks and never left the post for anything. Every payday he dressed in an expensive tailor-made white silk suit and a white dress shirt and a broad bright red silk necktie. He had bought the shirt and tie at an exclusive department store on one of his rare trips to town and the suit came from a Chinese tailor who served GIs from a small shop across the street from the base. On payday he left the post in a taxi and got out at an expensive restaurant called *Der Messerschmidt* and tipped the driver generously and went inside and ate an expensive meal with a bottle of champagne. After the meal of shrimp cocktail and fillet steak with a rich dessert he drank several shots of *kirschwasser*. He tipped the waiter generously and then he took a cab to one of the best whorehouses on the *Frauentorgraben* and engaged a woman for the night. In the morning he tipped his whore generously. He never engaged the same whore twice. After he left the whorehouse in a taxi he ate an elaborate brunch with more expensive champagne at a nearby hotel patronized by both German businessmen and American tourists. After the meal he sat at the hotel bar and sipped more *kirschwasser* and bought drinks for whoever happened to be there with him. Sometimes men at the bar thanked him and when it was a German Toon always told him the same thing: "I'm a rich American. It don't make any difference to me." When an American thanked him he always said, "No sweat, dude. I can afford it." He kept close mental track of his money and knew when he left the hotel bar that he had more than enough to pay the taxi fare back to the base. When he got off at the base he gave the taxi driver all the money he had and he would remain flat broke until next month's payday when he would do it all again.

The blood pounded in his temples and he was hot and then cold and shivering and suddenly hot once again. His abdominal muscles cramped painfully and he retched violently and then leaned back pressing his back hard against the packed dirt. Sitting that way he felt sealed into a hot, wet, dark, quickly shrinking world and he knew that the paydays in Germany were the happiest times he'd ever had.

GANDER AND KID KENTUCKY

Gander and Kid Kentucky were cousins who became hit-and-miss placer miners and after more than four years of nothing but miss they burrowed into the earth at this remote place. Deep into the mountainside in an ancient streambed they uncovered rich deposits including large nuggets of gold. The very first thing they did as rich men was replace their patched and stinking clothing and their sweat-stained hats and shabby boots. Two days after their return to their claim they were murdered by a roving band of seven Indians. The Indians never touched their gold and didn't even know about it and wouldn't have cared about it if they had known. They stripped the two men bare and were so happy with their loot that they didn't take time to mutilate the bodies. Weeks passed before Gander and Kid Kentucky were finally laid to rest by a preacher and his son in unmarked graves a short distance down the mountain from the mine.

EVERY LITTLE THING

Early the next morning in calm clear weather Rainbow headed south.

Eighteen miles from the Bird of Prey where a Forest Service road met the two-lane county road she picked up two hitchhikers. They were the same young couple that had visited the homeless shelter while Stones was sanding chairs in the early morning the day before.

When the boy and girl lifted their backpacks into the back of the van they looked at Uncle Sam on an air mattress underneath a red blanket.

"That's my husband," Rainbow explained. "He's disabled. He's asleep now. He travels better when he sleeps so I gave him some valerian this morning. Where you two headed?"

"North once we hit the freeway," the boy said.

"Thanks for stopping," said the girl.

"I'll get you to the freeway," Rainbow said, "but once we hit the freeway I'm heading south."

Back in the van the girl sat in the middle and the boy by the window on the front seat. All of them were slim so there was more than enough room. They knew they would soon part company and never see each other again and as often happens on the road they talked openly.

"You carrying weed in here?" the boy asked.

"No," Rainbow answered. "What makes you ask?"

"It smells a little like skunk."

"This van's been used for weed," Rainbow said. "Not by me though. But I guess I'm used to the smell." She wanted to change the subject. "Where are you two headed?"

"North," said the girl.

"Pretty far north," said the boy. "Where there's even less people than here."

"We're meeting some friends," said the girl. "We plan on living off the grid, completely."

"The civilized world's a mess," said the boy.

When they passed a small pond close beside the road a flock of wood ducks rose from the water and scattered in different directions through the trees.

"If you don't mind me asking," the girl said, "what happened to your husband?"

"The war," Rainbow answered.

"Shit!" the boy said. "See what I'm sayin' about the world? We're getting away from all the shit, that's all we want. We'll grow our own organic stuff, no more poisoned food. We'll get to breathe some really fresh air. No more crappy jobs for lousy pay. We got it all planned out."

"I have some friends up there," the girl said. "Kids I went to high school and college with. They've got a kind of commune going. It's not that structured. It's loose, but it's a lot like an old-time commune. Twenty-two people are there already. Sometimes the guys work part-time for the Forest Service, collecting seed cones from Douglas firs and stuff like that. But nobody works full-time. Nobody works more than they have to."

"I took off on my own when I was about your age," Rainbow said. "It's scary at first but you can make it. With a little luck you can."

"Where'd you run from?" asked the girl.

"Texas."

"Sounds like a good place to run from," said the boy.

"Want to hear some music?" Rainbow asked. "Bob Marley?"

"Sure," said the girl.

"Cool," said the boy.

Rainbow inserted the disc and they drove on through the trees. It was only ten more minutes to the freeway.

She pulled onto the shoulder just short of the on-ramp. After the boy and girl took their packs from the back of the van Rainbow handed the girl two fifty-dollar bills. "Good luck," she said.

"You sure?" the girl said. "That's a lot of money."

"I'm sure."

"Thank you!" said the girl. "It'll help us get started!"

"Thank you very much!" said the boy.

Rainbow thought about how Sunbeam had tried to escape the messed up world the boy had named by traveling north to this place and she wished the young couple luck farther north.

She felt almost peaceful once she was on the freeway headed south. The traffic was light and she stayed safely in the slow lane except when she had to pass a semitruck laboring up a hill. She had dug up her cash wrapped tightly in plastic and stored in coffee cans near the trunk of a sugar pine about a quarter mile up the hill across the road from the Bird of Prey. The secret place was what she called her land bank and now she could escape with more than enough money to resume life in a pleasant town where they had a school with a nursing program. For now that was as far as her plans for the future could go.

The fat deputy was alive and so was Sunbeam and she would be all right back at the Bird of Prey at least for now. Stones had survived and there might be others. There was a lot of wild country out there where everything had happened and no one knew exactly what had happened yet. It was likely no one would ever know exactly.

Half listening to Bob Marley, Rainbow thought about the fantastic force and unknowable power responsible for this fascinating mess of a world and all its transitory life.

On a long hill she passed one of those huge rigs loaded down with ten or a dozen shiny new cars. Were they Fords or Chevys or Volkswagens? She didn't know the difference and couldn't tell which and didn't care. Her van rode high enough so that as she passed the truck Rainbow glimpsed the ponytailed blond woman about her age who was driving.

Rainbow eased back into the slow lane ahead of the truck and glanced in the rearview mirror at Uncle Sam riding feet-first and laid out on his back atop the air mattress and covered up to his neck with the clean red blanket. The next rest stop she remembered should appear inside two or three miles and Rainbow would stop and park in the back of the lot where the trucks parked and would give Uncle Sam water and food if he was awake and seemed to want it. Then she would clean him and change his pad and talk to him and maybe he would blink his eyes.

She would take care of Uncle Sam for as long as he lived or as long as she did. There was no way she could know but from what she could sense Uncle Sam seemed all right about the move. After she talked to him she would lock the van with the windows cracked and walk a few laps around the rest area for fresh air and exercise. Inevitably there would be panhandlers and she would smile and hand each of them a five-dollar bill. Or a ten. Or a twenty when she knew for certain one was a vet. Veterans Day would be here soon.

Bob Marley's signature song began.

In the back of the van Uncle Sam sensed the rhythm and hum of tires on the smooth road underneath them but he couldn't hear Bob Marley.

> *"Hold the pickles, hold the lettuce,*
> *special orders don't upset us…"*

That was all Uncle Sam would ever hear anywhere.